Snatched

from

Innocence

Lisa George

Lisa George

ISBN 978-1-64349-286-5 (paperback)
ISBN 978-1-64349-287-2 (digital)

Christian Faith Publishing, Inc.
832 Park Avenue
Meadville, PA 16335
www.christianfaithpublishing.com

Printed in the United States of America

First and foremost, I want to thank God for His help and inspiration in writing this novel. Without Him, it would not have been possible.

Secondly, I want to thank my Mother, Hilda George. What a privilege and blessing it was to have her work with me. I'm so grateful for her wisdom and patience and with her help this book is complete.

Thirdly, sincere thanks go to my dear friend Marilyn Spurrell, who also remained by my side. With her insightfulness, she provided help and encouragement to produce this finished product.

Chapter 1

It was a day when the July sun would not relent in its intensity. The vegetable garden had suffered due to the drought conditions that had begun earlier that month. Harvest time was approaching, but the vegetables were failing to grow to the desired product the Saunders were hoping for. Rain would have been a welcomed blessing, but the heavens refused to comply. Life wasn't easy for the little family. Brett and Rachel Saunders tried their best to provide and care for their two children, twelve- year old Adalyn and eight- year old Caleb. Out of work for a year and employment insurance benefits exhausted, Brett searched for job possibilities but was unsuccessful. As a stay-at-home mom, Rachel toyed with the idea of working outside the home to help with the financial burden while Brett was unemployed.

Adalyn's room felt like a furnace as the sun beamed in through her window. Sitting at her desk reading her latest library book, her head began to thump as her face reddened from the heat's exposure. With her wavy, brown hair dangling down past her shoulder blades, she decided to tie it up in a ponytail to reduce its warmth, as it invaded her neck. Opening the window in hope of a breeze, she glanced out to witness her dad's tall stride as he walked toward her mom. Working in the vegetable garden, Brett had looked up long enough to notice the brooding expression on his wife's face. Wiping her brow with her forearm as she expelled a puff of air from her lips, fatigue was making an appearance on her petite frame. With downcast eyes she continued mulching to compensate for the lack of water produced by the drought conditions.

"Rachel honey, what's wrong?" he asked, kneeling down beside her.

"Brett, I can't do this anymore!" she answered, shaking her head as her eyes filled with tears from the sound of his voice.

"Do what?" he questioned, trying to make sense of what she was talking about as his eyebrows lifted in intensity, forming deep lines into his forehead.

"This! All of it! This garden is so difficult to maintain without water. I know we are doing our best, but I'm tired Brett, so tired! What are we going to do?" She sobbed, unable to look at him.

"Rachel, sweetie, it's okay, harvest season will soon be here and all the hard work will have been worth it."

"No Brett, it's not going to be okay, don't you understand?" She finally peeped up in hope that he would offer some form of understanding.

"Understand what, Rachel?" he asked, not perceiving that there were additional things on her mind.

"Brett, do you realize that our savings are nearly spent?"

"Our savings?" he asked himself while scratching his head. "Weren't we just talking about the garden?"

"We are quickly running out of money," she continued, "what are we going to do when it's all gone?"

Pausing for a moment, a huge sigh escaped him as he placed his left hand under her chin to lift her face toward him. "Rachel, look at me," he urged.

Gazing into his captivating blue eyes, she was mesmerized, as her cares melted away as per his usual effect on her, *even* after fourteen years of marriage.

"I know it looks bad, Rachel, but we *will* get through this. I'm confident, I will find work soon. Please don't worry, you can trust me, Rachel. It will all work out."

Not totally convinced with his answer, she lowered her head and nodded.

"Come here," he motioned, as he reached for her.

Snuggling into his arms, she enjoyed the sturdiness of his embrace. It reminded her of his inner strength and reliability that he had *always* demonstrated the eighteen years she had known him.

"Mom, Dad, where are you?" Caleb shouted, startling them both.

"Here we are," Brett yelled back, releasing his grip on Rachel.

Standing to their feet, Rachel quickly wiped her face of the tears and brushed the dirt from her jeans.

"How was your sleepover at Spencer's?" Brett asked, rubbing Caleb's head, tousling his dark brown hair.

"It was a lot of fun, but I missed you, guys," came his reply. Time apart from them was always kept to a minimum.

"What are *you* guys doing?"

"We are working at this vegetable garden, would you like to help?" Brett invited, offering him the trowel.

"No way," he replied, shaking his head. "I hate vegetables."

"Oh yeah!" Brett said with a smirk as he picked up the water hose.

"Daaaad! What are you doing with that?" he asked as his eyes popped at Brett with the same hue of brown as his mother's.

"Come here and I'll show you," he replied as he aimed at Caleb dousing him with water.

"Ahh, I'm soaked." He laughed, running away from his father.

Brett is such a good father, Rachel thought as she laughed at them both having fun. *He loved teasing both Adalyn and Caleb, and they enjoyed every minute of it.*

"Caleb, where's Adalyn?"

"In her room, Mom, reading, as usual," he yelled back as he wrestled Brett for the water hose.

Heading up to the house, she caught a look of playfulness on Brett's face from the corner of her eye, and as she turned to face them, she knew what was coming next.

"Don't you dare!" she warned, tiptoeing backward.

"Let's get her, Caleb!" Brett yelled, running toward her.

Screaming as she darted for the house, she ran inside just in time to escape getting showered by the water hose.

"Adalyn," she called out, placing her gardening gloves onto the washer.

"Yes, Mom?"

"It's a beautiful day outside, do you want to come out and have some fun? Dad and Caleb are having a water fight with the hose," she said with a hint of joy in her voice.

"No thanks, Mom, I want to finish reading my library book before I have to take it back."

Adalyn loved reading so much so that she yearned for it and spent countless hours soaking up every word. She planned to be an English professor at a prestige university one day, just like her momma's sister, Quinn, who was teaching at the University of Saskatchewan.

As the exact opposite of her, Caleb hated school and everything involved with it. Summer holidays were the best time of year he had always said.

"Adalyn, do you have all your chores done?"

"Yes, I do, Mom," she answered from her bedroom, not looking up from the page in the book she was reading.

Unsurprised at her daughter's answer, Rachel knew both Adalyn and Caleb had always completed their chores as told. Although they had their ups and downs, she was blessed to have such a great family; of course no family is perfect, but they had raised their children to be respectable to them *and* to others. Giving them suitable chores to be completed each day. Life wasn't handing out free passes, and they had to learn the value of honest work at an early age.

"Adalyn, can you help me with dinner?" Rachel asked as she began peeling the potatoes.

"Coming, Momma," she replied reluctantly, closing the book's cover and moving to the kitchen.

Soaking wet and dripping water all over the floor, Brett and Caleb appeared in the kitchen.

"Ahh! You guys, you're getting water all over my clean floor, go and change," Rachel scolded.

"Sorry, Mom," Caleb apologized as he headed for his room, dripping water all the way in.

Sneaking over and grabbing Adalyn, Brett squeezed her into a bear hug, soaking her *as well* with his wet clothes.

"Daddy! Get away from me." She laughed, struggling to break free from his grasp.

Spinning around, he noticed an *armed* Rachel with a potato in each hand ready for combat. "Don't you dare!" she warned chuckling, ready to release if he intended to give her the same type of hug.

"Okay! Okay! Cease fire!" He laughed with hands in the air. "I'll go and change."

Standing at the kitchen sink, Rachel washed the peeled potatoes for a salad she had planned for dinner, and placing the last of the vegetable scraps into the garbage bag, Adalyn offered to bring it outside to its bin. Watching her from the window, Rachel noticed a man leaning against a tree from across the road as he appeared to be staring in Adalyn's direction. Starting to feel unsettled, Rachel turned to locate Brett but quickly glanced outside again to find the stranger had disappeared. *That was weird!* she thought, shrugging her shoulders. *My eyes must have been playing tricks on me*, she continued as she finished preparing the meal.

*****

Returning with dry clothes and ready to give Rachel a kiss on the cheek, Brett noticed the faucet.

"Is that thing still leaking?" he asked, fiddling with the sprout.

"Yes, remember I told you about it last week."

"Yeah, I must have forgotten it. I'll be right back," he promised as he stepped outside and into his shed to retrieve his toolbox.

"Brett, that will have to wait, dinner is ready," she informed him upon his return.

"Okay, I'll fix it later, I can't miss out on your momma's chicken," he replied, winking at Adalyn.

"Yes, Daddy," she agreed." Momma is the best cook."

"Caleb! Dinner is ready," Rachel shouted, lodging his plate on the table.

Bowing their heads, they waited as Rachel gave thanks for the meal they were about to eat.

"Dig in!" Brett commanded as he picked up a chicken leg.

"Daddy, tell us how you and Momma met," Adalyn asked in between bites.

"Sure! I love telling that story!"

Chapter 2

"It was June month, and I had just graduated from high school," Brett began. "I was eighteen and ready to take on the world, but I had one *problem,*" he stated with his index finger in the air.

"What was that, Dad?" Caleb asked.

"I was broke!" he replied in a deep firm voice as they all laughed.

"Peterson's Grocery and Convenience Store needed a worker for the summer, and I saw my chance. They hired me on the spot because of my *good looks* and *charm.*" He chuckled with a wink.

"Yeah right, Dad!" Caleb argued, screwing up his nose.

"I *believe* it, Daddy," Adalyn piped in with a grin that showed everyone her perfect white sparkling teeth and a twinkle of mischief in her eye.

"Yeah, *you* would . . . Daddy's little girl," Caleb teased.

"Now! Now! Both of you listen," Rachel interrupted, "please continue, Brett."

"Where was I? Oh yeah . . . the store. I worked at the beginning of summer, planning to stay a few months and then move to a *larger* city to make the *big bucks.*"

"How long *did* you work there?" Adalyn asked as she took a gulp of her juice.

"Three years! The whole time I was dating your mother." He smiled as he glanced lovingly at Rachel.

"Tell us how you met! Tell us how you met!" they both chimed in together.

"*Your* mom was seventeen and one of the popular girls, but she didn't know I existed. I had seen her around town once in a while, but I kept my distance. She was always with her friend Claire."

"I was working at the store one day when your mom walked in. Boy oh boy was she ever beautiful!"

"Yuck!" Caleb expressed disgustingly, "I don't want to hear that lovey dovey stuff. I'm going in on my iPad."

"Did you have enough for dinner?" Rachel asked, sipping on a mouthful of tea.

"Yes," he yelled out, already in his room.

"Keep going, Daddy, I want to hear it," Adalyn encouraged, looking at him through her striking, deep-set blue eyes.

"At the back of the store, someone had dropped a can of pop, breaking it open all over the floor. I was mopping it up when she walked in. She didn't see me at first, and her long bouncy brown hair was all messed up from the wind. I couldn't help but smile as she quickly fixed it, looking around to see if anyone had spotted her."

"Momma, you *still* do that," Adalyn pointed out, laughing.

"I can't help it." Rachel giggled. "I embarrass easily."

"I watched her every move as she walked to the cooler to pick up a carton of eggs and over to the bakery section to get some bread," he continued.

"Brett! You were *staring*!" Rachel interrupted with a *you-know-I'm-right* look on her face.

"Yeah . . . It's true." He nodded. "I *was* staring."

"I finished mopping up the mess and decided to go up to the cash for a chance to talk to her. I was so nervous, Adalyn. As I began to walk up, my foot hooked into the mop bucket and I went sprawling onto the floor."

"Oh no, Daddy! Did Mom see you?"

"Oh, Adalyn!" he said, shaking his head. "When I opened my eyes, I saw two feet in front of me. As I slowly looked up, there was your mom smiling down at me."

"Are you okay?" she asked kindly with her hand up to her mouth, trying her best not to laugh.

"I sprang to my feet *faster* than I had fallen. Yes, yes, I'm fine, I answered, but Adalyn"—he laughed—"my face was redder than the deep red lipstick poor Mrs. Bensen wears at church, bless her soul!" he continued as Adalyn burst into laughter.

"Now what was I going to do? The prettiest girl in town saw me when I fell. 'That old bucket is always in the way,' I uttered, as she looked at me with those big brown warm eyes. 'Can I help you with anything?' I asked trying to ease the situation. 'I'm ready to pay for my things now,' she replied with a smile that told me I would be thinking about her for the rest of the night, and by that time, Adalyn, even the tips of my ears were red. 'Thank you, have a nice day,' I said as she left the store. I cannot believe I just fell down in front of Rachel Anderson! I thought to myself."

"Momma what did you think of Daddy?" She now turned her attention to Rachel with enthusiasm in her voice.

"I had never noticed him before," Rachel answered, "in *fact* I didn't even know who he was. I felt so embarrassed for him when he tripped and fell, but when I paid for my things, I saw how cute he was."

"Then what?" Adalyn asked intrigued, as she placed her chin in both hands and lodged her elbows on the table.

"Well, I loved his coal black hair and muscles." She giggled, but I didn't have time for a boyfriend. I was reading all the time, like you, Adalyn. I wanted to finish school and focus my attention on becoming an editor at a book publishing company."

"Momma, you didn't get the chance to do that!" she whined, feeling sorry for her mother.

"That's okay, my life took a better turn. I wouldn't trade it for anything." She smiled.

"I didn't have time for a boyfriend as I just said," Rachel continued, "but I couldn't stop thinking about him. I asked Claire who he was, and she told me his name was Brett Saunders. We didn't see him around much because he was too quiet and shy. So . . . if I wanted to see him again, I would have to go back to Peterson's store."

"Did you go, Mom?"

"Yes, I did, a few days later when Nanny Anderson needed some flour. It was my chance, so I volunteered to go. Looking through the store window, I watched Daddy help Mrs. Walker, an elderly woman, pick up the items she needed. He seems like a nice guy, I thought."

"That's my daddy!" She gleamed with a sparkle in her eye.

"Thanks, sweetheart," he replied, kissing Adalyn on the forehead.

"Did you know she was outside, Dad?"

"No, and I didn't even see her when she first walked in. I was busy behind the counter stocking the bins with candy when I turned around and saw her.

"It's her! I thought to myself. Don't stare! Do not stare! Oh, but I couldn't help it. She was the prettiest thing I had ever seen. As she walked toward the counter, I began fiddling with the cash register so she wouldn't notice how nervous I was.

"'Hello, Brett is it?' she asked me, laying the flour on the counter.

"Her gorgeous brown eyes stared at me as I attempted to answer. 'Yes that's correct,' I replied with a little crack in my voice . . . So embarrassing Adalyn, so embarrassing!" he said, shaking his head.

"'It's a nice day out there. When do you get off work?' Momma asked still smiling.

"'In a couple of hours,' I answered, clearing my throat.

"'That's good,' she replied, 'at least you will be able to enjoy the last of the sunshine.' Placing the flour in a bag, I tried to get the nerve to ask her if she would like to see a movie sometime; but I was quickly losing confidence.

"'By the way my name is Rachel,' she called out leaving the store. I smiled and thought to myself, it was now or never!

"'Hey, Rachel'

"'Yes?'

"'Would you like to see a movie sometime?'

"'Sure, I would love to. Here's my number, give me a call,' she replied, writing the number on a piece of napkin, before leaving the store. Three years flew by so quickly as we dated. I continued working at Peterson's, and your mom finished high school and decided to go to the college in North Battleford. I wanted to ask your mom to marry me, and it was all I had thought about since our first date. I had saved most of the money that I made at the grocery store, and I'd been looking at a small house down on Baileys street. It needed some work, but I could do most of it myself and it had a huge piece of land for us to grow our own vegetables. I'd started working with the new construction company here in town as a carpenter's aid, and I knew it would be a good living for us."

"How did you do it, Daddy? How did you ask momma to marry you?"

"Ted Lewis owned a small farm outside of Battleford. On the weekends, during the winter, he gave free sleigh rides to the children. Your mom kept asking me to take her for a ride, but I always had an excuse not to go. As I thought of a way to propose, I realized that a sleigh ride would be perfect."

"Momma, were you excited?"

"I didn't know about it because it was a surprise."

"Tell me more, Daddy."

"I called and made plans with her for that night and instructed her to dress warm. She was very curious, but I kept it a secret." He winked.

"I picked her up at 7:00 at night and drove to Ted's farm."

"I screamed so loud because I was finally going on a sleigh ride." Rachel laughed.

"It was a beautiful clear night," she continued, her eyes glazing over as she reminisced. "We could see our breath from the cold frosty air. Daddy wrapped a blanket around my legs to keep me warm, but it was so romantic, Adalyn, that the cold didn't bother me.

"The snow along the trail that led us away from the farm was so pretty, Adalyn. It was glistening like diamonds under the silvery moonlight. I wish I had taken a picture of the evergreen trees with their branches laden down with the powdery snow. Oh, Adalyn! It was perfect!" Rachel expressed as she remembered every detail of that night. "As I turned to look at Daddy, I found him staring at me with the sweetest smile. I realized at that *precise* moment *just* how much I loved him."

Adalyn's eyes widened even more as she listened to her mom tell the story.

"'Brett, where are we?' I asked as we left the main trail, stopping at a log cabin.

"'This is Dad's cabin,' he replied. 'He hasn't used it in a long time.'

"'Why are we here? Tonight?'

"'Come on, you'll see,' he answered.

"Daddy opened the door and walked in behind me. A fire was smoldering in the fireplace, and I could feel it's warmth as I stared in amazement. He stoked the embers of it and placed another log on, and soon it was blazing again.

"Putting his arm around me, he gave me a quick kiss on the cheek and invited me to sit next to him on a rug in front of the fireplace. I could see his hands shaking.

"With the fire crackling in front of us, he took my hand and looked me in the eye. 'Rachel,' he began, 'there's something I want to say to you.'

"'Yes Brett?'

"'I need you to know how much I love you and how much you mean to me.'

"Then Daddy took my hand and helped me up, and guess what came next, Adalyn?"

"He asked you! He asked you to marry him!" she exclaimed excitedly.

"Yes, he bent down on one knee and opened the box and showed me the ring and said, 'If you will be my wife, you will make me the happiest man alive. Will you marry me?'

"I was speechless. I loved that man so much! Of course, I wanted to marry him.

"'Yes, Brett, yes, I will marry you. I would be proud to be your wife. I love you too.'

"A big smile came on his face as he grabbed me and gave me the biggest hug. We snuggled by the fire talking and laughing until we realized it was time to get back. We had good news, and we couldn't wait to tell. We both wanted a small wedding, so we invited a few friends and close family. We didn't have a lot of money, but we were happy. As long as we were together, we knew everything would work out."

"You didn't live in the big city like you planned, Daddy?"

"I didn't want to go after I met your mother. I was happy living in Battleford. Your mother preferred living in a smaller town also rather than a big city like North Battleford, so we built our house here."

"Besides," Rachel piped in, "if we needed anything in the city, it was only ten minutes away."

"I like it here too," Adalyn replied.

"Two years after we were married, *you* came along, Adalyn." Rachel beamed. "Our hearts were filled with so much love, and we thought it couldn't get any better. Then, along came Caleb, and our world was complete. Life was and still is perfect."

"That's a nice love story," Adalyn pointed out. "I love my family."

"We love you and Caleb too," Rachel replied, "more than you will ever know."

"I want to be just like you, Momma, when I grow up and meet a handsome prince like you, Daddy."

"You will, sweetheart, *one* day . . . But for now I want you to stay my little girl for as long as you can."

"Okay, Daddy!" she agreed as she wrapped both arms around his neck, giving him a big squeeze.

"It's time to clean up from dinner," Rachel announced, getting up from the table.

"I can help you with the dishes, Momma," Adalyn offered as she began picking up the forks.

"I'll be back to fix that faucet," Brett shouted on the way out the door.

Rachel watched as he left and once again became anxious. Times were getting worrisome, and with no money coming in, they were in big financial trouble. Due to shortage of work, the construction company he had been working for let him go and that was a year ago! Brett was *persistent* if he was anything. Each day, he searched for a job opportunity and vowed he would never give up until he found *something*.

Outside, walking toward his car, Brett detected the motion of someone within his peripheral vision. Quickly turning, he caught a glimpse of a figure lurking through the shadows but was unable to distinguish the identity. Thinking it was only a man out for a walk, he dismissed the perturbed feeling that surrounded him and stepped inside his vehicle.

*****

The next morning, Adalyn and Caleb were still fast asleep at eleven o'clock when Rachel arrived home from her appointment.

Walking into the house, she took a deep breath. The remainder of the coffee she had brewed that morning was sitting on the countertop. It's aroma, she had once *loved,* was now making her nauseous. She noticed a bead of sweat trickling down Brett's forehead as he worked on fixing the kitchen faucet. She could hear the frustration in his voice as he struggled to free a bolt and hesitated to tell him the news but decided to share with him anyway.

"Brett, I'm home from the doctor and I have something to tell you!"

Placing the vice grips on the stand, he turned around and looked at her pale face. "What is it, honey?"

Chapter 3

"For the past couple of months," Rachel began, "I've been very nauseous and vomiting constantly. My energy level has not been up to par. With everything going on around here, I didn't notice the changes that were happening to me. I became suspicious one day after throwing up for the third time that morning."

"Rachel, what are you saying?" he asked, walking toward her.

"I had a checkup with my doctor this morning and found out that we are . . ."

"Having another baby?" he yelled, finishing her sentence.

"Yes! We are having another baby!" she screamed with her hands in the air with excitement.

"When?" he asked, reaching down and wrapping her in his arms as he swung her around the kitchen.

"We are due on February 4," she replied, catching her breath.

"That only gives us a little over six months to get everything ready! We need the crib taken out, we need a nursery started. Oh boy! We need more room!"

"Hold on there, sweetie, let's take this one day at a time." Rachel giggled.

Standing beside her, Brett rubbed his head as plans for a new baby began to surge through his mind.

"Don't worry, Brett!" Rachel reassured as she noticed him staring at the floor, beginning to pace a little. "We have a lot of time to get things ready."

"Sorry, honey, for a minute there, I thought the baby was coming next week." He chuckled.

Although overjoyed with the expectation of a new baby, Rachel couldn't help but concern herself with their income, or *lack* of it! How would they care for a new little one? If Brett didn't find a job soon, she planned to talk to him about going to work as a housekeeper at one of the hotels in North Battleford.

At that instance Adalyn and Caleb walked into the kitchen and noticed the huge grin on Brett's face as they caught a glimpse of their mother running for the bathroom with her hand up to her mouth.

"What's going on?" they questioned in unison.

"You're going to be a big sister, and Caleb, you're going to be a big brother," Brett answered, quickly swiping his eyes as to not let them see his tears.

"What's wrong, Daddy?" Noticing his actions. "What do you mean?"

"You are going to have a new little brother or sister."

"A new baby?" Caleb exclaimed.

"Yes, a new baby," Rachel replied as she reappeared.

"When?"

"Next February."

"Oh, I can't wait! That's a long time away, Momma!" Adalyn pointed out.

"Yes, it is, but that will give us time to prepare the nursery."

"Can I help with it?" she asked, eager to start.

"Yes, you can when the time comes, but for now, can you peel the carrots for supper?"

"Oh, Mom!" she complained. "I was planning to go to the library."

"I need you here, Adalyn!"

"Please, Momma, my literature books are overdue and I want to take out a few more."

"How old are you anyway, twelve or thirty?" Rachel sighed. "How do you understand it all?"

"I don't know." She laughed, shrugging her shoulders. "I'm really interested in it, maybe that helps."

"Okay, you can go. Brett, can you drive our daughter to the library?"

"Yes, sure. I need a part for the faucet, so I'll drop her off on the way to the hardware store. Are you coming too, Caleb?"

"Yep!" he replied, heading out to the car.

"I love you, Momma, thank you." Adalyn smiled as she kissed her on the cheek.

"Hmm mmm." Rachel laughed.

Grabbing the greasy rag from his back pocket, Brett wiped his forehead as he looked at Adalyn grinning.

"Oh no, you don't, daddy! Get that greasy rag away from me," she protested with her hands up to stop him.

As he ran toward her, she scrambled out the door laughing, but was too fast for him as he chased her around the backyard. "You win," he shouted, bending over gasping for his breath. "Let's go to the library."

"I'll pick you up at 4:30 p.m., okay?" Brett said as they drove into the library parking lot.

"Yes, okay! Love you, guys. See ya, Caleb," she shouted, slamming the car door.

*****

After returning her books, Adalyn went searching for more, and sitting to a nearby table, she noticed a strange man staring at her.

"Hello, my name is John," the man introduced himself, walking to her table. "I'm sorry for staring at you, but you remind me so much of my granddaughter. You *look* about her age too."

"What's her name?" she asked with her eyes fixated on the floor.

"Anna, she's twelve and a half. How old are you?"

"I'm twelve as well, sir."

"What's your name?" he asked, not taking his eyes from her.

"Adalyn"

"Well, Adalyn, it was very nice to meet you." He smiled as she returned to her table to finish reading.

*****

20

Pulling into the hardware store, Brett noticed his friend, Pete Lambert, stepping out of his SUV.

"Hey, Brett. Hi, Caleb. I haven't seen *you two* in a long time," he stated, walking toward them.

"Hi, Pete, yeah, it's been a while!"

"What have you been up to?"

"Not much, Pete. House repairs keep me busy, and we just found out that we are expecting!" He beamed with excitement.

"That's great news, Brett. How is Rachel doing?"

"She's fine except for the morning sickness."

"Yeah, I hear it can be awful," Pete agreed as his brown eyes squinted with the thought of pain.

"How about you?" Brett asked. "What is it like to be a detective?"

"It's great! Very rewarding, you have good days and bad days, but the good outweighs the bad."

"Yeah, I hear you." Brett nodded. "I know where you're coming from."

"It's quiet here in Battleford. There's isn't much action in a small town like this. It's just the way Mya likes it." Pete laughed, stroking his light brown neatly cut hair.

"Yes, Rachel would share the same concerns. It's good you have a job you enjoy."

"How about you? Have you found anything?" Pete asked, standing strappingly tall as he took an oversized mouthful from his coffee cup.

"No! I'm searching every day, but nothing has come up," he replied as he began to pace a little.

"Don't lose hope, Brett. I'll pray for you as well."

"Thanks, I have to run, I'll catch up with you later," he responded, heading to the store's entrance. "Let's go, Caleb."

"Call me some time, we can get together for a coffee," Pete shouted, holding his cup in the air.

Shaking his head, Brett walked away. *Pete is a good man,* he thought, *but this God stuff? I mean, I know God is up there somewhere, but really? Praying for me to get a job? I can find that on my own.*

Pondering the conversation they just had, Pete knew that whenever God was mentioned, Brett couldn't walk away fast enough. *One day*, he thought, *Brett would see just how good God really is.*

*****

I'll be there in five minutes, Brett's text stated as Adalyn looked up. Already four twenty, she gathered up her backpack and went outside to wait for him.

"Hey, Daddy." She smiled, throwing her bag in the back seat, almost hitting Caleb.

"HEY! Watch out!" he yelled, glaring at her.

"Oh, sorry, I didn't mean to do that," she apologized.

"Hi, sweetheart," Brett interrupted. "What did you read about today?"

"I was reading about Anne of *Green Gables* today, Daddy, and I met a nice man there too."

"What are you talking about, Adalyn?" he asked, turning toward her as his eyes scrunched, drawing his eyebrows closer together.

"A man at the library came over talking to me and told me I looked like his granddaughter."

"Adalyn, I told you before not to talk to strangers!"

"Oh, Dad! This is a small town, don't worry so much."

"I don't care how small the town is, you need to be careful, sweetie."

"Okay, Dad," she said, rolling her eyes at him.

"And watch that attitude," he said sternly.

"Yes, Daddy, I'm sorry," she apologized as they arrived home.

*****

The following day was a scorcher with the temperature reading 32°C, and rain was nowhere in sight. Due to the continual stress of the drought and their lack of income, Rachel suffered from daily headaches. Persevering in the job search, Brett remained unsuccessful. North Battleford offered no assistance either, with their construction companies hiring their same crew each year, making it impossible to find work in that type of field. Needing to provide for his family, Brett knew he would have to look for a different job title. Despite their troubles, however, Brett and Rachel ensured their children didn't know as much.

Eating the last of her spaghetti, Adalyn heard a text coming through her phone. *Hey, let's go swimming*, her best friend, Haley, suggested.

I was planning to go to the library, she texted back, *you should come with me.*

No way! Haley replied. *I hate reading, and it's too hot to stay inside.*

I don't know, Adalyn texted back.

We haven't hung out in a long time. Come swimming with me pleaaaaase! LOL.

All right, I'll go.

I'll ask Mom to take us, Haley responded.

*****

"Hi, Mrs. Perkins."

"Hi, Adalyn, are you ready to go swimming?" She smiled, looking back at her.

"Yeah, Haley talked me into it." She laughed as she buckled her seatbelt.

"Wow, there are a lot of families here," Haley observed as they pulled into the park.

Placing a blanket on the grass, Mrs. Perkins sat down with her favorite book, *Pride and Prejudice*, and instructed the girls to be careful as they ran for the water.

Quickly jumping in and escaping the sun's hot rays, they found themselves refreshed. Glad she had made the decision to go swimming with Haley, Adalyn realized that she spent a lot of time reading in her room and at the library and Haley missed her. In fact, she missed Haley just as much. They enjoyed the afternoon swimming, laughing, and being best friends.

"Haley, Adalyn! It's time to go," Mrs. Perkins shouted as suppertime was approaching.

"Ahh, Mom, do we have to?" Haley yelled, still in the water.

"Yes, I have to get supper ready," she replied, picking up her blanket.

"We have to go, Adalyn, Mom is calling."

"Coming," Adalyn yelled, swimming in.

Walking toward the car, Adalyn caught a glimpse of the man from the library and a woman, who she thought may have been his wife.

"Hello," she greeted, putting up her hand.

"Hi Adalyn." He waved back.

"Who's that?" Haley asked, getting into her car.

"His name is John, I met him at the library yesterday, but I don't know the woman who is with him."

"Why were you talking to him?" she questioned with a puzzled look on her face as her eyebrows raised.

"He told me that I reminded him of his granddaughter. We only spoke a few minutes."

Watching them place their towels in the trunk, Haley noticed that his license plate number contained the first two initials as her mom's and said as much to Adalyn.

"Yeah, you're right, it does," she answered as they both laughed.

Spending the rest of the night outside on their front bridge, Adalyn and her family sat around telling stories, laughing at each other's jokes, and enjoying the warm breeze on their faces.

*****

Awakened to the sound of birds chirping outside her window, Adalyn looked out to find a blue jay bird perched on the ledge, but it quickly flew away from the rattling as she tried to open the window. High in the sky, the sun beamed down, but they needed rain badly. With the smell of eggs cooking, she was lured to the kitchen to find her mother preparing breakfast.

"Good morning, Momma, where's Dad and Caleb?" she inquired as she stretched and made a loud yawning noise.

"Good morning, sweetie. They're outside cleaning the car before the sun gets too hot."

"Can Daddy take me to the library after breakfast?" she asked, sitting down to the table ready to eat her mother's delicious fried eggs.

"Again today? It's a really nice day, don't you want to spend it outdoors?"

"Yes, maybe after lunch, but I really need to finish this book and its quieter at the library."

"Okay, ask him when he comes in," she replied, taking the bread out from the toaster.

*****

Thirty minutes had passed when Adalyn noticed John walking into the library. *This man is* everywhere, she thought as he nodded and sat to a nearby table.

"You must really enjoy reading?" John asked, standing next to her.

"What?" she jittered, looking at him puzzled.

"Sorry, I didn't mean to startle you," he confessed. "Most young people are out having fun during the summer."

"Yeah." She laughed. "I *do* spend a lot of time here."

"My wife and I recently opened a used bookstore, and I buy the books which are no longer needed here," he said, anticipating her interest.

"Oh really? I'd love to come by one day with Mom and Dad," she responded as her curiosity peeked.

"Do you have a cell phone? I could text you the address."

"Yes, I do, but I'm not allowed to give my number out to strangers."

"Yes, I understand," he said, smiling. "I'll write it on this piece of paper for you."

"Thank you, John. I'm going to ask Momma as soon as I get home."

"See you then," he called as he gathered his books and left, thinking his mission was accomplished.

*****

That's odd, Brett thought as he found Adalyn waiting outside on the library steps for him to pick her up for lunch. *I usually have to text her to come out.*

Opening the car door to get in, she began talking immediately, rambling on and on.

"Slow down, pumpkin."

"Daddy, there's a new bookstore opened in town! It's *used* books, but I don`t care, books are books, can we go please? Today?" she asked earnestly with her hands clasped as if in a begging position.

"We can't go today because we are busy at the house, but we can take you in a couple of days."

"Thanks, Daddy, you're the best!" She grinned, reaching up to give him a kiss on the cheek.

"I didn't know that a new store opened in town, how did *you* find out about it?" he asked as he signaled to make the turn onto their street.

"My new friend, John, and his wife opened it."

"Your *new friend*, John? Who is John?" he continued his inquiry.

"Remember, Daddy, the man I met at the library the other day."

"I told you, Adalyn, to be careful talking to strangers!"

"He's not a stranger, Daddy. I've spoken to him a few times now. He's really nice," she tried to rectify the situation.

"Did you say that he is married?"

"Yes, Daddy, and they have a granddaughter *my* age, her name is Anna," she answered, letting out a sigh at all the questions.

"I'll talk to your mother about it, but I don't think it will be a problem," he replied as an enormous smile formed on Adalyn's face.

*****

"Come on, guys, what's taking so long?" she shouted, trying to hurry them as the time finally arrived for her to go after waiting two long days, which felt like two weeks.

"Adalyn, it's only a bookstore!

"Mom!" She gasped. "I can't believe you just said that!"

"I'm teasing," Rachel replied, laughing.

"Bennett's Used Books," she read aloud on the big white sign over the door as they drove into the parking lot. She couldn't wait to get in there!

Chapter 4

——◦◦◦◦◦◦——

Bursting in through the door of the bookstore, Adalyn began inspecting the place as she gazed around at all the books that were before her.

Eyeing a tall older man behind the counter, Rachel noticed he was neatly dressed and wearing glasses. *Is this the man who was taking interest in her daughter?* she asked herself as her thoughts were confirmed when he introduced himself.

"Hi, my name is John, you must be Adalyn's parents?"

Who is this man? Rachel thought suspiciously. *He addressed us like he's Adalyn's new best friend, and I've seen him somewhere before but I can't recall where.*

"Yes, we are, it's nice to meet you," Brett replied, shaking his hand.

"And who is this little guy?"

"My name is Caleb," he replied confidently.

"It's nice to meet you, Caleb," John answered, giving him a high five.

Crash! Jumping at the sound of books falling in the back room, they all stood motionless waiting for John's explanation.

"That's my wife, Sophia, let me introduce you to her. Honey, can you come out here for a minute, I want you to meet some people."

Appearing around the corner, a slightly shorter woman looking to be in her early fifties greeted them.

"Hi, I'm Sophia Bennett." She smiled. "Sorry about the noise, I was *attempting* to do two things at once."

Shaking hands, they talked for a bit while Adalyn scouted out the store. Money saved from her allowance enabled her to buy two books that were going at a bargain.

*****

On the drive home, Rachel told Adalyn how John had invited them all for supper the following night.

"See, Daddy, I told you he was a nice man, no need to worry."

"I'm not totally convinced yet," Rachel piped in, shaking her head at Adalyn.

"He is really nice, Momma, you'll see if we go to their house for dinner."

"It will be rude I suppose if we don't go," Rachel pondered, looking out her window.

"Yes, it will and I suggest that we go," Brett replied, nodding. "It's only a meal!"

*****

Honestly, that girl, I can't believe how much she loves to read," Rachel shook her head as Adalyn ran straight to her room with the books upon returning home.

"Rachel! Do you hear yourself? You were exactly like her when you were her age."

"Yes, I remember. All I wanted to do was lock myself in my room reading, while my friends were out enjoying themselves. And now Adalyn is just like me. It's good that she loves to read, Brett, but I fear she is going to miss out on the fun of being a teenager."

"She'll be okay, Rachel! If she grows into the woman that *you* are, then she will have both brains *and* looks." He winked.

"Oh, Brett! You still know how to make me blush." She smiled sheepishly with her hand up to her face.

"I hope she gets a man as good as the one you have," he teased.

"I know how blessed I am, you don't have to remind me." She laughed with her arms folded.

"I love you, Rach!" He squeezed as he took her into his arms. "Don't ever forget it!"

"I love you too, Brett."

*****

The following day brought a lower temperature of 24°C and clear blue skies. Although she had enjoyed reading her books, which she had purchased at the bookstore, she decided today to hang out with Haley again. Until that day at the park, she had forgotten how much fun they had together. A delighted Haley, with her long blonde curly hair swept up tightly within a clip, spent the day outside with her as they practiced cartwheels, handstands, and other techniques for their gymnastics team at school.

Watching from the kitchen window as they jumped around enjoying their time together, Rachel was glad Adalyn found such a good friend in Haley, and she cherished every moment that her children were happy.

*****

"Brett! Caleb!" Rachel shouted for them as they worked on fixing Caleb's pedal bike out in the shed. "We are leaving for the Bennett's soon. Come in and wash up!"

Remaining a little skeptical, she refused to be impolite on their invitation to supper. Believing that *one* should not go empty-handed when invited out for a meal, she baked a chocolate cake, and with it in hand, they headed off.

Meeting them at the door, Sophia greeted them with a big smile and a hug, and after thanking Rachel for the cake, she invited them in.

"Hello, Mr. and Mrs. Saunders, Adalyn, and Caleb, it's nice to see you again," John stated, shaking their hands. "Come to the living area and sit while we wait for supper to be ready." Looking around, Adalyn found that it wasn't a big house, but everything was in its *place* and it smelled of freshly cut flowers.

Pot roast, mashed potatoes, and baby carrots, all tasted good, as they enjoyed their meal. *The lady is a great cook*, Caleb thought to himself, *but not as good as Mom*!

Ending the meal with the cake Rachel had brought, they then moved the conversation into the living area.

As parents to a boy and girl, John and Sophia had suffered the devastating loss of their daughter in a boating accident at the age of ten. They enjoyed, however, their times as grandparents to the four children of their son.

With her heart crumbling, Rachel listened to their story of heartbreak over losing their little girl. Although it was twenty years ago, time had been kind to them and they coped a little better as each day passed.

Turning the conversation to a brighter note, John began telling them how Sophia and himself moved to Battleford to open their own business.

"Brett, we need someone to help around the shop a couple of hours a day," John stated, "not a real job, but just replacing books, sweeping the floor, and keeping things tidy. I think Adalyn would be perfect for it. It will only be a little spending money for her, and she can read whenever we are not busy."

"Oh, I don't know, John," Brett replied. "Adalyn is only twelve. I won't let her help out unless one of us is with her."

"I understand completely. Sophia will be there the exact time as Adalyn, and you can be confident that she will watch her like her own child. In fact, she's a little overprotective since the accident. So you really don't need to worry."

"Please, Daddy! I'll be extra careful. Sophia will be there to watch me. I can do the job I know I can. I've been doing chores since I've been eight, so I can totally do it."

"I don't know, sweetheart. Your mother and I have to talk it over."

"There's no pressure Brett, just let me know, and she can start on Monday. I'll hold the spot until then."

As Rachel helped Sophia with the dishes, Brett and John continued talking. Squirming in her chair, Adalyn became restless with each exciting thought entering her mind about John's proposal to help out at his shop. *Hurry, Mom and Dad*, she thought, *we need to get home so you can talk about my job opportunity.*

*****

"Momma, please convince Daddy to let me do this," Adalyn pleaded in the car on their way home.

"I don't know, Adalyn, you have to give us time to think about this. We will give you an answer by Friday. John said he would hold the position for you until he hears from us."

"Okay, Momma, but let me say *one more thing*! I can help out a little around the house with the money I make," she suggested, thinking they would surely allow her after hearing that comment.

"Adalyn! That's very kind of you to offer, but don't ever think that you have to *work* to help us. Your mom and I will take care of everything. You don't have to worry about things like that."

"Sorry, Daddy. I thought I could help in some way. I hear you guys talking, and I know we are in trouble."

"Your dad will find work soon, Adalyn."

"Yes, Momma," she replied with her head down, fearing they would say no to John's offer.

*****

Placing the last of Brett's shirts into the washer, Rachel considered Adalyn helping out at John's store. Friday had arrived too quickly for her, and today, they had to make a decision.

"Rachel, what is our answer regarding Adalyn?" Brett asked as he walked into the laundry room.

"I don't know, Brett. It's all I've thought about since John asked us. It's only two hours, but I *can't* shake this uneasy feeling I have. I know how much she wants to do this, but my instincts are screaming NO!"

"She's our little girl. It's natural for you to be scared, but I will take her myself and pick her up right after. Adalyn is a good girl, Rachel. She would enjoy helping out so much."

"Yes, I suppose. Maybe I *am* worrying too much. What can happen at a bookstore? This town is pretty quiet," she stated with her hand on her hip.

"I'll go tell her the good news." Brett smiled as he left to find Adalyn.

"Thank you, Daddy! Thank you, thank you!" Adalyn shouted with delight as she wrapped her arms around his neck, giving him a big kiss on his cheek.

"Your mother is in the laundry room, go say thank you to her as well."

"I will, Daddy." She beamed as she headed towards the room.

*****

With Sunday as designated church day, the Saunders kept *tradition* by attending and giving God thanks for all His kindness to them.

Dressed in their best attire, they sat in their usual seats, about halfway up from the back. Forgetting where they were for the moment, Adalyn and Caleb began to laugh as they watched funny videos on Caleb's phone, resulting in Rachel giving them one of her *looks* that told them to stop and pay attention. Noticing the blank stare on her dad's face, Adalyn knew *he* wasn't paying attention, so she wondered why *they* had to.

Looking around at the church's full capacity, she watched as people fanned themselves to obtain relief from the hot and humid weather. Restless, the children wiggled in their seats, as the older men wiped the sweat from their brow with their handkerchief.

Soaking up every word, Rachel listened as the preacher spoke about God's protection and provision. Unable to hide her doubts, her saddened eyes closed in despair as she thought about their situation.

Why did *they go to church every Sunday?* Adalyn thought. *Was it out of duty? What was it all about?* Was she too young to know this *God* they were talking about?"

"What's wrong, Momma? Why are you crying?" Adalyn whispered as she witnessed a tear escape her eye and trickle down her cheek.

"It's mommy stuff, nothing to concern yourself with, sweetheart."

Glancing over her shoulder, Adalyn noticed a *funny* look on Pete Lambert's face as he looked at Brett. Recognizing him as her dad's friend, she wondered why he was looking their way.

"Good morning, Brett, good to see you again." Pete smiled, shaking his hand as they all began to leave after the service was over. "How are you?"

"I'm okay, except for the job hunt, it doesn't look promising, Pete. I'm doing my best to stay positive for my family, but they are starting to see my struggle. The stress is *too* much for Rachel."

"Have you talked to the pastor about it? He can ask the church to pray for you guys."

"No, not really! I come to church, but I can't say that I have much faith in all this."

"Brett, I was in your same position a few years ago before I started at the Police Academy. Food was in short supply causing us to question our next meal. I put my faith and trust in God, and He came through for us. Meals were brought to us daily by different people."

"I don't know, Pete." Brett shrugged. "Wasn't that just a coincidence? People knew you were in need and supplied the meals?"

"That's it though, Brett, our God supplies *all* our needs, and He likes to use people to accomplish it. Two months I had been out of work before the opportunity came to attend the Police Academy. I would not have chosen that particular career choice, but I felt really strong to apply. When God closes one door, He opens another one."

"I have to go, my family is waiting for me," Brett replied, looking over at Rachel. "I'll catch up with you later."

"Call me anytime," Pete shouted.

Watching Brett as he joined his family, Pete decided that he would be available for whenever Brett needed to talk.

*****

"Are you all right, honey?" Brett asked, noticing how quiet Rachel was on their way home.

"I'm thinking about what the pastor was saying this morning. How God provides and protects. I can't help but wonder where your job is. It has been a whole year, Brett!"

"Rachel, listen to me, I *will* find a job, you can depend on me. It's good to go to church, but we live in a *real* world where we provide for ourselves. I will find a job!"

As another tear fell, she turned away. If she didn't have *church* to hope in, what else was there?

*****

Rachel prepared ham sandwiches and pink lemonade for lunch, which they enjoyed on the front patio. With the wind changing direction, it caused the temperature to drop a few degrees, and as dark clouds rolled in, Adalyn felt a splash on her nose.

"Momma, I think I felt rain! Was that rain? Momma!" she cried excitedly.

It is *getting darker*, she thought, looking up at the sky. Unable to express her thoughts of going inside, the heavens broke apart. Producing the needed rain they had been waiting for, it first began with large splashes and then magnified into torrents.

"Come on, we need to go inside before we get soaked," Rachel yelled. Looking behind her, she began to laugh as Caleb ran and jumped in the puddles that had already formed in the grass while Adalyn did cartwheels again. Running back to her children, Rachel joined in the fun.

"Thank You, God." She laughed. He had finally *sent* the rain, and their vegetables were going to make it.

*****

Thirty minutes before the sound of her alarm, Adalyn woke at nine o'clock, Monday morning. John was expecting her at the shop at eleven, and she needed to be ready.

*****

"Adalyn, please listen to Sophia and be watchful of strangers," Rachel instructed on the way to the bookstore.

"I will, Momma, don't worry."

As Brett, Rachel, *and* Caleb accompanied her inside the store, Sophia reassured them of Adalyn's safety and to pick her up at one in the afternoon and with continued concerns and denying her instincts, Rachel gave her a hug as Brett kissed her on the forehead.

"See you at one," they both stated.

"Okay, I love you," she yelled, watching them drive out of sight.

Instructing her to step inside, John shut and locked the door.

Chapter 5

Standing by the window, John looked out to ensure Brett and Rachel were nowhere in sight before making his move.

"Let's go!" he demanded, grabbing Adalyn's arm and snatching her cell phone from her hand.

"What? John, what are you doing? Where are you taking me?" she uttered as tears began to form.

"You're *ours* now little one." Sophia sneered as she walked out from the back room.

"What do you mean?" Adalyn cried, looking at her.

"We are going to make a ton of money from you," Sophia continued, ignoring her cries.

Having no idea of what was transpiring, Adalyn's stomach became queasy. As her face turned pasty and unable to stop, she vomited all over John's leather shoes.

"Now look what you've done!" He growled. "Take her Sophia! We have to move quickly."

"Where are you taking me?" she asked with tears streaming down her face.

"Don't worry your pretty little head about the details. Now stop asking questions!"

Grabbing Adalyn's arm, Sophia placed a dirty chloroform-soaked rag over her mouth. Struggling for her breath, she inhaled the substance. After five minutes, the room began to spin and her body relaxed as she lost consciousness.

"Okay, John, she's out, hurry we only have a short window here."

"I'll take her to the car," he shouted, "get your stuff together and meet me out there, the guys will get the rest of it."

"I'll be there in a minute."

"Don't be long, Sophia, we have to move."

Before heading out the door, she did a final check for her belongings, but she failed to notice the coffee cup sitting on the window sill.

"Sophia!" John shouted from the car. "Let's go!"

As John changed the gears, she jumped in the car and they sped away, leaving Battleford behind and taking Adalyn with them.

After driving fifteen minutes, Adalyn began to regain consciousness.

"Where am I?" she asked, looking around the car.

"She's awake, John," Sophia announced, glancing back at her.

"Wh-where are you taking me?" she stammered.

"Don't answer her, Soph!" John interrupted. "Turn around and keep quiet! She's just a price tag now!"

Adalyn moaned as her head throbbed with pain. Still disoriented, her focus turned to her hands, and she suddenly became aware of the fact that she was tied to the handles of the door.

Flashbacks appeared before her eyes as she began to remember what had happened just thirty minutes ago.

"Stop!" she yelled. "You can't do this! Bring me back home!"

"Be quiet out there!" Sophia snapped as her eyes flashed a signal of contempt for her.

Pulling and twisting at the rope that was binding her, in an attempt to free herself, she found it was useless; the rope was tied too tight. "Let me go!" she screamed. "Untie me! You can't do this!" she cried over and over again.

"Keep quiet out there!" John yelled, staring angrily at her through the rearview mirror.

Sobbing, she looked out the window. Attempting to figure out where they were going, nothing seemed familiar to her. Although knowing they had left Battleford, the only thing before her were trees and long stretches of road.

Looking again in his rearview mirror, John noticed Adalyn peering through the window. Realizing she would discover where they were as she read the road signs, he pulled the car over to the side.

"Get out there, Sophia, and put a blindfold on her," he ordered.

Quickly obeying, she opened the door next to Adalyn and tied a scarf around her head to cover her eyes.

"Sophia, please stop," she begged. "Bring me home."

"You better keep your mouth shut for the rest of the trip," she warned as Adalyn screamed from the sting of Sophia's hand as she slapped her hard. *Who are these vicious people?* she thought to herself. *What are they planning?* she cried quietly as for them not to hear her. She knew she was kidnapped, but *where* was she going?

Pulling onto the highway again, John proceeded toward their destination. Still suffering from the effects of the chloroform, Adalyn became woozy and thought her head would burst from so much pressure.

Silent for a long time as they drove for what seemed like hours, Adalyn sat quietly in the back seat with no idea where they were. Pulling into the entrance of a hiking trail, the car came to a stop.

Exiting the car, John and Sophia met with the person who gave them directions to Adalyn's *buyer.*

"Help me please! Somebody help me!" she screamed, hoping someone out there would hear and come to her rescue. Listening as footsteps approached the car, she heard the door to her left open and a strong smell of cheap cologne found her nose.

"Hello," she whimpered, not able to see due to the scarf. "Please, mister, can you help me?"

Upon her request, she felt a hard slap across her face again. Scratching her with his ring, it left a cut on her right cheek. "Stop screaming or I'll hit you again," his voice echoed in her ear as she yelled out in pain.

Trembling with fear, she realized it wasn't John, because this voice was a lot deeper and forceful.

Reaching over, he cut the rope that tied her to the handles and grabbed her hair. "Get out of the car," he ordered.

Dragging her from one vehicle to the other, he then slammed her onto the floor of a van. Waiting inside, John and Sophia wrapped duct tape around her arms, thus restraining her.

"How old is she?" the man questioned.

"Twelve," answered Sophia.

"Seth will be waiting for you at the turning point. Twelve-year-old girls are a good market. He'll pay good money for her."

She was being sold! Listening to their conversation, Adalyn panicked as she desperately attempted to free herself from the restraints of the duct tape. Inhaling too quickly and frequently, she began to hyperventilate, resulting in lightheadedness as she struggled to breathe. Realizing what was happening to her, she managed to slow her breathing as she began to calm herself.

"Please, Sophia don't do this," she pleaded again as they drove away. "You're a nice lady. You don't need to do this!"

"Be quiet!" John's voice shouted back at her.

As she continued screaming, John became furious, slammed on the brakes and pulled over again.

"I'll keep you quiet one way or the other," he yelled. "If you can't follow simple instructions, then you'll learn the hard way."

"What was he going to do?" she feared. Forcing a powdery substance into her mouth along with a mouthful of water, he answered her question.

As her eyes began to get heavy, her head bobbed up and down. Unable to fight it anymore, she succumbed to its effects. They sped away as she laid unconscious on the floor of the van.

*****

Another six and a half hours of driving had occurred before Adalyn woke again. Unable to see, she remembered the scarf was blocking her vision. Missing her family immensely, she yearned for them as she subconsciously agreed with their concerns, regarding allowing her to help out at that bookstore. Why didn't she listen?

Hearing Sophia mumbling to herself, she surmised that John had left the van and strained her ears to hear what was being said outside.

"Are you Seth?" John asked yet another stranger.

"Yes, I am," he squirmed, looking around.

"I have a package here for you."

"What's the age and nationality?"

"A twelve-year-old, white Canadian female," John replied.

"$15,000 is what I can give you." He stood with his head high glaring at John.

"Hey, man," John snickered, "I know how much Canadian girls are worth, I'll take nothing less than $25,000!"

"No! No! I cannot pay that much," Seth answered, shaking his head

"The deal is off, I'll take her to someone who can," John replied confidently.

"Okay! Okay! Wait, I will pay the amount you want," Seth relented.

Momma and Daddy will never find me, Adalyn thought gasping. *I'll be lost forever! Daddy I need you!* she cried before drifting off into unconsciousness again.

*****

Driving to the store to pick up Adalyn, Brett felt the knots in his stomach tighten. Rachel *already* had an uneasy feeling about the whole situation, and now it was *his* turn. *Why had we let her do this?* he asked himself as insecurity invaded his thoughts. Maybe he *was* overreacting, after all, it was just a bookstore in a small town. What could happen? Allowing her to help out at the shop with the agreement that Sophia would be personally responsible for her, had been unknowingly misconstrued and was somewhat unnerving for him. Receiving no reply from a text he had sent, he hoped the reasoning was that she had been too busy to respond.

Finally arriving at the store, he leaped out of his vehicle. Taking two steps at a time, he reached the handle and opened the door.

"What is going on?" He stared in disbelief as the blood drained from his face.

Chapter 6

———◦◦———

Standing in the doorway of the bookstore, Brett stared at the emptiness that was before him. Lacking their books, the shelving on each wall caused a perplexed emotion within him. As his eyes flicked over the area, he discovered the chairs occupying the opposite corners of the space closest to the door and the sectional couch, which once sat in the middle of the floor, were all removed. As well, the check-in counter, which lay across the far left corner, along with the plants that were scattered throughout the shelving and the store, were also taken away.

"Adalyn! Adalyn! Where are you?" he yelled, racing toward the backroom to find *it* abandoned as well.

Silence!

"Where is she?" he demanded to know as he stood in the center of the store so engrossed in her absence that he continuously encircled the space, producing the same ineffective result. Adalyn was not in the building!

"John! Sophia! Where is everyone?" he shouted, bewildered at the situation as a cold sweat developed over his body when he realized no one was responding.

"Adalyn honey, answer Daddy, come on, sweetie, you're scaring me. Where are you?"

A trembling father struggled with the dreaded thoughts of having lost his daughter. The fear that most dads acquire but pray will never happen. The pounding of his heart against his chest was so loud in his ear that he was fearful of not hearing her if she called for him.

Maybe they're outside, he thought, failing to recognize the deserted parking lot when he first arrived.

Running out of the store in an uncivilized scurry, he searched the perimeter around the building and found no one. "Where is she? Adalyn, where are you!" he yelled, scrutinizing the area.

The neighbors may know something, he thought upon catching a woman peeping out from behind her curtain, watching him flail about.

"Yes, may I help you?" she asked with the door partly ajar fearing what he may do.

"My name is Brett Saunders," he said, panting for his breath. "I dropped my daughter off at that bookstore 11:00 this morning. When I came back to pick her up, she was gone. Do you know the owners of the shop, John and Sophia Bennett? Have you seen anyone leave there today?"

"Yes, I did!" she answered, fully opening the door. "The couple renting the building had a little girl with them. I assumed she was asleep because the man carried her out to the car in his arms."

Pacing the lady's front porch, Brett rubbed his head. "Do you know the owner of the building?" he asked, struggling to breathe.

"Yeah, it's Daniel Weber. He lives on Fairmount Crescent, number 4 I think."

"Okay, thanks," he replied, running down her steps and jumping into his car.

Not exactly sure where it was, he entered the address into the maps on his cell and arrived in Mr. Weber's driveway within four minutes.

"Yes, can I help you?" An elderly man appeared as he opened his door.

"Hello, are you Mr. Weber?"

"Yes, I am, what can I do for you?"

"I understand you own a building on Cedar Lane?"

"Yes, that is correct," he nodded. "What's this about?"

"I'm inquiring about the couple who owned the bookstore there," Brett stated as he moved nervously about the man's property.

"Yes, John and Sophia, lovely couple."

"The couple are gone, sir, and they've taken my little girl!" Brett stared at him hoping for answers.

Scratching his head, Mr. Weber asked Brett to continue.

"I dropped my daughter, Adalyn, off at the store two hours ago. When I came back to pick her up, she was gone. They had taken her."

"No, that can't be right!" Mr. Weber shook his head in disbelief. "John paid me cash for one month rent for the bookstore space *and* for the house they rented from me. He told me he was starting up a little bookstore business for him and his wife. They were semi-retired but needed a little extra money to get by."

"Yes, he told me the same story," Brett concurred.

"Did you say they are gone?" Mr. Weber asked as his eyebrows arched in confusion.

"Yes, sir, they are, and they have my daughter. I'm sorry, but I have to go."

Driving home *faster* than he should, questions raced through his mind. *Why did they take her? Where were they going with her?* They had no money, so it couldn't be for a ransom. He had to find her. "Adalyn honey, Daddy will find you, just hang on!"

*****

"Rachel! Rachel, where are you?" he called, bursting open the door.

"I'm here, Brett, what's wrong?" she asked, detecting immediately by the tone of his voice that something was amiss. "Where's Adalyn?"

"She's gone Rachel, they've taken her!"

"What are you talking about, Brett?" Her wobbly voice stung him as he was about to tell her that he had lost their daughter.

"I drove to the bookstore to pick up Adalyn, but she wasn't there."

"What do you mean, she wasn't there!" Rachel snapped as her tone changed from fear to anger. "She *has* to be there!"

"No, Rachel, she's not! John and Sophia took her. They've emptied the store and disappeared!"

"They can't be gone Brett, they must be somewhere, you probably didn't see them!" she reasoned.

"You're not listening to me, Rachel!" he yelled, grabbing her shoulders. "They have kidnapped Adalyn! We have to call 911," he exclaimed as reality suddenly sunk in.

"No! Not Adalyn, my precious little girl!" she howled, falling to her knees. "This can't be true, please, God, don't let it be true."

Dialing 911, Brett waited for the dispatcher to answer.

"911, what is your emergency?"

"My daughter has been kidnapped. Please send someone, hurry!"

"What is your location, sir?"

"10 Bailey's Street, Battleford."

"What is her name?"

"Adalyn Saunders."

"And your name, sir?"

"Brett Saunders."

"How old is your daughter?"

"Twelve, she's twelve years old."

"What was she wearing?"

"Ah, Rach, what was Adalyn wearing?" he asked as his voice quivered.

Crying so loud, she didn't hear his question.

"Rachel!" he shouted, "what was she wearing?"

"Black shorts, pink top, and flip flops," she mumbled, thinking back to earlier that morning.

"When did you last see her?"

"At 11:00 this morning, I dropped her off at a bookstore here in town to help out this couple we know."

"What is the couple's name and the name of the store?"

As he proceeded to give the dispatcher the information, Rachel bolted for the bathroom. Already weak from her morning sickness, this added stress intensified the nausea as her facial features turned horribly pale.

"An officer will be there within minutes," the dispatcher informed Brett.

Returning from the bathroom, Rachel found him pacing the floor.

"Rachel honey, are you okay? You look awful! Come and sit to the table," he invited.

"How do you think I'm doing?" she lashed, giving him one of her *I-can't-believe-you-just-said-that-to-me* looks. "My daughter has been stolen!"

"The police are on their way, please try and stay calm for the baby."

"Don't tell me to stay calm, Brett! They have my Adalyn. They have my girl!"

"I know, Rachel, but we have to stay focused for her. We need to tell the officers everything we can remember to help find her."

"I knew we shouldn't have let her go to that shop. She's too young. I don't care if it was *just helping out*! I had a bad feeling about it from the beginning. Why didn't I listen to my instincts? Now she's gone," she cried, toppling into the recliner with her face in her hands and elbows on her knees, rocking back and forth.

Startled by the officer's knock, Brett ran to open the door.

"Hello, officers, please come in."

"I'm Detective Owen Smith, and this is Detective Pete Lambert. We've been assigned to your case."

"My name is Brett Saunders, and this is my wife Rachel," he replied, shaking the detective's hand.

"Hello, Mrs. Saunders." He nodded as he greeted her, but with watery eyes and mascara running down her cheeks, she could only give him a blank stare.

"Brett! What is going on?" Pete asked with concern.

"It's our worst nightmare, Pete, the Bennett couple kidnapped Adalyn."

"Okay," Detective Smith interrupted. "Let's start from the beginning," he suggested, standing superior to everyone as a husky, barrel-chested mountain of a man.

Reiterating the horrifying story of what had happened just an hour ago, Brett and Rachel educated the detectives with each and every last remembered detail.

"Rachel, where's Caleb?" Brett asked as he made his seventh trip encircling the coffee table.

"Here I am, Dad," he announced, coming out of his room.

"What's goin' on, Mom?"

"You need to go back in your room, son, until we are finished talking to the police."

"Police? Why are they here?" he questioned. "Where's Adalyn?"

"We will explain it all to you after the police leave," Rachel replied. "I'm sorry, Caleb, please go to your room and wait."

"Mr. and Mrs. Saunders, what kind of relationship do you have with your daughter?" Detective Smith questioned. "Is it a healthy one? Do you fight or argue?"

"We have a great relationship with her, Detective, a scatter argument here and there, but nothing serious. Just the usual twelve-year-old stuff."

"Does she have a boyfriend?"

"No, sir, not that we are aware of."

"How about the computer? How much time does she spend on that?"

"Look, Detective! Adalyn is a good girl! An honor student. She doesn't spend a lot of time on the computer because she is reading most of her time. She is obedient and completes all her chores without any trouble. Haley Perkins is her best friend. and they hang out whenever they can."

"I'm sorry, Mr. Saunders, but I need to ask those questions in order to gather all the bits of information I can. Is there a chance she could have run away?"

"No, never!" he answered with a degree of irritability as he closed his eyes and pinched the bridge of his nose. "We are a close family."

"Do you have a recent picture of her?"

"Yes, we do, I will go get it for you," Rachel said as she staggered into her room.

"We need to put out an 'Amber Alert' for her right away. It has only been a couple of hours since she went missing, maybe someone has spotted her."

As Rachel gave Adalyn's picture to Detective Smith, Brett revealed the rest of her information.

"Can you describe the couple that you believe abducted her?"

As Brett described John and Sophia, Rachel listened with disbelief. How was this happening? How could their lives be turned upside down in just a few hours? Where was she? Were they hurting her?

"Can you think of anything that may have happened over the past few months that was unusual?" Detective Smith asked.

"I remember seeing a man standing next to a tree from across the road, and it looked like he was watching Adalyn one night when she carried out the garbage," Rachel stated. "He was only there a few seconds and then he disappeared. I thought my eyes were playing tricks on me, so I didn't pay much attention to it."

"Yes, something similar happened to me too," Brett recollected as he told them his experience with a stranger lurking around their property.

"We will place an 'Amber Alert' for her as soon as we get to the station," Detective Smith promised. "We will also investigate John and Sophia Bennett and anything else we can find. We'll keep in touch."

"I'm so sorry for all this," Pete sympathized. "I'll be praying for you."

"Thanks, Pete."

"Remember, Brett, you can trust God, He can bring her back home to you."

"Please do whatever you can to find her," Brett begged.

As Brett shut the door behind him, Pete's words played over in his mind. What if they *don't* find her? What would they do? They may *have* to call on 'Pete's God' to help them. The same God Pete was sure would save Adalyn and deliver his family from this nightmare.

"This is all your fault, Brett! You talked me into letting her go!" Rachel glared as he turned to face her.

"This was not my fault, Rachel, it was both our decision."

"*I'll bring her and pick her up myself,* you said! *Sophia will be watching her,* you said. If it wasn't for *you*, she would still be here!" she scowled.

"Rachel, how was I supposed to know they were going to take her? We've met them, they appeared to be nice people."

"You should have listened to me, Brett! I told you my instincts were saying no. Our little girl is gone, and it's all your fault!" she shouted on her way to their bedroom.

"Rachel, stop it! It's nobody's fault!" he answered, unable to believe what he was hearing. "We have to pull ourselves together and concentrate on finding her."

"Just leave me alone, Brett!" she yelled, slamming the door.

Wow! Just give her time to cool off, he thought, *she's upset.*

Picking up the phone, he called both sets of parents to fill them in on what had happened, and within minutes they were at the house.

"Come in, everyone," he motioned. "Rachel is in the bedroom, devastated." Myles and Daisy Anderson rushed to the room to help console her as Mr. and Mrs. Saunders lingered in the living room.

"Caleb," Brett called, "can you come out here, son? We need to talk to you."

Walking from his bedroom, Caleb felt something was wrong. Sitting down next to his grandfather, Brett explained the situation about Adalyn.

"I want Adalyn to come home!" He cried after hearing that someone had taken his sister.

"I know, son, the police are out looking for her," Brett reassured, kneeling down beside him.

"I DON'T CARE!" he screamed. "I want her to come home NOW!" He wailed as he ran to his mother's side.

"How are *you* holding up, son?" Mr. Saunders asked as he watched Brett stand with his eyes closed, stroking his temple.

"I don't know, Dad, I feel helpless, I can't just sit around here waiting, I need to do something, I have to get out of here! I need to go look for her."

"Wait, son, you can't go out alone, you're not thinking straight. We'll come with you."

"I'll let Rachel's parents know where we're going and ask them if they can stay," Brett replied, heading toward the bedroom.

Chapter 7

Detectives Owen Smith and Pete Lambert pulled into the police parking lot. As Owen entered his office, a huge sigh escaped him because he hated cases like this where the child went missing. It was heart wrenching to see what both parties had to endure. With three kids of his own, that kind of fear was always present in his mind. Although maintaining professionalism, he sympathized with the parents and vowed that he would do all he could to help find her.

"Detective Smith," Pete shouted, "I have a message for you from a man by the name of Daniel Weber. He left his number for you to call him."

"Thanks, Pete, I'll call him after I've issued an 'Amber Alert' for the little girl."

Owen typed in the information:

Saskatchewan Province Amber Alert in effect
Please contact Detective Owen Smith at 555-0130 or dial 911
Child: White female, twelve years of age, thin build, long brown hair and blue color eyes.
Wearing black shorts, pink t-shirt and flip flops with a flower design

Abductors: White male, 5'10", late 50s, salt and pepper hair color.
Medium build and wearing glasses

Wearing black dress pants and light blue dress shirt

White female, 5'7", early 50s, shoulder-length brown hair

Thin build, wearing white capris and red top.

Believed to be driving a 2010 dark blue Chrysler Sebring

After issuing the 'alert,' Owen dialed Daniel Weber's number.

"Hello, this is Detective Smith, you left a message for me to call you?"

"Yes, Detective. I own a building on Cedar Lane in which I had rented out to John and Sophia Bennett, who operated a bookstore. They also rented a house from me and paid cash for a month rent for both places and were excellent tenants. A man came by my house today stating they took his little girl."

"What was the man's name?"

"I don't know, Detective. He left in such a hurry I forgot to ask him, but he did say his daughter's name was Adalyn."

"Did he say anything else?"

"Only that the store was cleared out and they were gone. I didn't go down there yet because I wanted to check with you first."

"That's good thinking, Mr. Weber. We have to investigate the space for evidence."

"Did the couple give you a reference when they first applied for the building?"

"Yes, sir. When I called to check it out, the man told me they were a great couple, who always paid their rent on time and were no trouble. In fact, he hated to see them go."

"What was the name?" he asked, writing the information in his notepad.

"I'll have to go and get it for you," he replied, dropping the phone hard onto his table and producing a resounding noise in Owen's ear.

"Okay, sir, I'm back. The name is Justin Campbell."

"When you called Justin for a reference, did he tell you what line of work he was in?" he asked, switching the phone to his other ear.

"Yes, he did, he was a lawyer who owned a building in downtown Saskatoon. John had rented a space in that building for three years. He told Justin they were tired of the city and was moving to a quiet town."

"Do you have a phone number?"

"Yes, it's 555-0165."

"Is there anything else you can tell me about them?"

"No, not that I can think of right now, Detective. The only time I saw them was the day they paid rent. They didn't cause me any trouble, so I had no need to be in contact with them."

"Thank you for your cooperation. If you think of anything else, please let me know."

"Yes, I will, sir. I hope you find that little girl."

"You and me both, have a good day."

As Detective Smith hung up the phone, he turned to his computer and brought up the police database to find out what he could on John and Sophia.

Not present in the system, Owen thought it strange for them to be absent of a parking ticket and surmised they used fake names to carry out their plan.

Rummaging through the papers on his desk, he found Justin Campbell's number and made the call, and as he hung up the phone, Owen shook his head upon discovering the number belonged to a payphone in North Battleford.

They were clever people, he thought. *Justin was a fake reference.* Running his name through the database, he had no success in finding him.

"Pete, we need to talk to the people living next to the bookstore. Hopefully someone can give us a clue."

"Let's go," Pete replied, already on his way to the door

*****

"Yes, may I help you?" A woman appeared who lived in the house next to the bookstore.

Showing his badge, Owen introduced them. "Hi, ma'am, we are with the Battleford Police Department. My name is Detective Smith, and this is Detective Lambert. We need to ask you a few questions about the couple who rented that bookstore."

"Yes, would you like to come in?"

Following her to the kitchen, she offered them a cup of coffee.

"No, thanks," Owen replied. "We won't be taking up too much of your time, just a few simple questions."

"Can you describe the couple?"

"The man was tall. He wore glasses and his hair was black with streaks of gray all over, you know like the salt and pepper style? The woman was a little shorter than him and very thin. Her hair was brown until today."

"What do you mean?" Pete asked.

"She was blond when I saw her this morning. She either dyed it or it was a wig. I had to look twice because I thought it was another woman."

"What time did you see them today?"

"Earlier this morning around 11:30. They left the store with a little girl. She was asleep because the man brought her out in his arms. The woman came running out a few minutes later, and they drove off."

"Can you describe the little girl?"

"She was a petite little thing with long, brown hair. Probably around eleven or twelve years old," she answered as she gestured with hand movements.

"Did you notice what she was wearing?"

"Yeah. Black shorts and a pink top."

"That's good information." Owen nodded as *her* countenance brightened from becoming *pleased* with herself.

"Did you see what kind of car they were driving?"

"No, I'm not good with the make and model of cars, but I *do* know it was a four-door, dark blue one."

"Anybody else show up there that you can remember?"

"Yes, fifteen minutes later, two men came in a large pickup truck and loaded up all the books. I thought it was strange because they were only opened a month. They moved rather quickly, and within forty-five minutes they were gone. Then later, a man showed up asking questions," she continued.

"When?" Owen asked her.

"Around 1:10 p.m. He was beside himself, pacing back and forth, rubbing his head. I think he was the girl's father. Is that little girl missing or in trouble, Detective?"

"Yes, we believe so. There is an Amber Alert out for her. So if you think of anything else, please call the station."

Letting themselves out, they drove straight to the police head-quarters. Remaining quiet, Pete had a bad feeling about it as he pondered all the information they had. For one mere moment, he couldn't help but think the worst for Adalyn and that they would never find her; but saying a quick prayer, it removed the doubt once again.

"We need to investigate the bookstore," Owen said, interrupting Pete's thoughts, "but first we need a warrant. I'll call Kari Rhodes when we get back to the station."

*****

"Hello, District Attorney Kari Rhodes speaking."

"Hi, Ms. Rhodes, Detective Smith here."

"Yes, Detective, what can I do for you?"

"I need a search warrant to investigate a bookstore here in town involving the alleged kidnapping of a twelve-year-old girl."

"I need a reason, Detective," she said, standing up from her desk, perceiving this was a serious case. "You know Judge Watkins, he requires a good rationale."

"I have an eye witness stating she saw the alleged couple taking a little girl that matches Adalyn's description."

"That's not really enough, Detective, it could have been *their* child."

"The telephone number of the reference the alleged couple gave to the owner of the building belongs to a payphone in North Battleford, so I believe they used a fake reference. We need to search that building, time is of the essence. She's only twelve, Ms. Rhodes," he stated as she listened intently to the rest of the details.

"I'll do up the paperwork," she consented. "You'll have to come by my office and sign the affidavit."

"Will do," Owen replied.

A couple hours later with an appeal to Judge Watkins and all the paper work finalized, the warrant was issued.

"Pete, let's go!"

"Right behind you, sir."

"Upon arriving at the bookstore, they observed the empty parking lot. The unlocked door opened up to a vacant building."

"They left in a hurry!" Pete stated, looking around at the desolation.

First searching the main area of the shop, Owen immediately spotted the coffee cup on the window sill.

"Pete, look what I have here." He smiled as he bagged it.

"The rest of the shop was notably clean, and upon inspection of the backroom, Owen was convinced that he wasn't going to find anything else on his own."

"Pete, call forensics in North Battleford and tell them to meet us here ASAP."

*****

Arriving back at the station, Owen sent the cup straight to the lab.

"Hey, Veronica," he greeted as she looked up from her microscope.

"Hi, Detective, what can I do for you?"

"I need you to analyze this coffee cup, and I need a rush on it."

"I'll try my best," she answered, taking the item from his hand.

"Thanks, call my office when its ready."

"I will," she nodded.

Returning to his office, he decided to call Brett and fill him in on what had occurred since their last conversation and to obtain the Bennett's home address from him.

*****

Spending hours driving around, Brett and his parents combed every street and side road, searching the park, local businesses, ponds, and wherever they could think of looking. Feeling helpless and running out of options to finding her, they decided to head back to the house. "What was he going to do?" Brett asked himself as his mind reeled with questions and assumptions. "How was he going to find Adalyn?" He had no clue where they had gone. As far as he knew, they could be in another province by now!

Pulling into the driveway, they could hear the sound of someone crying from within the house.

"Is that Rachel?" Mrs. Saunders asked, staring at her son with eyebrows raised, flabbergasted to be able to hear her outside.

"Yes, Mom, it is. The stress of losing Adalyn is too much for her, *and* she's three months pregnant. I don't know what to do for her!"

"Just be there for her, son. Understand that her frustrations are not aimed at you. You don't have to *fix* everything, sometimes all she'll need is a listening ear and a shoulder to cry on."

"I can do that." Brett nodded, closing his eyes in despair. "Mom, we have to find her. She's my little princess, Daddy's girl," he continued as he broke down crying.

"I know, son. She means everything to all of us. Stay hopeful. The police will do all they can to find her."

Brett agreed and suggested they go inside.

They found Mr. Anderson and Caleb in the kitchen getting a glass of water.

"Hi, Brett, how are you holding up?" Mr. Anderson asked, laying a hand on Brett's shoulder.

"Hey, Myles, I'm not doing so good. We've been all over Battleford looking, but there's no sign of her. I don't know what else to do. How's Rachel?"

"She hasn't stopped crying since you left. Daisy has been in with her, but nothing seems to work."

"Okay, thank you for all your help," he said as he looked at Caleb.

"Daddy, where's Adalyn? Why haven't they found her yet?" he asked, crying.

"I don't know, son, the police are doing everything they can, we have to let them do their job. Try not to be afraid, we'll find her."

"I miss her, Dad, I want her to come home."

"Me too, son! We all miss her," Brett replied, hugging him.

Crying for several minutes in his father's arms, Brett finally released him.

"I have to see Mom now, okay?"

"Yes," Caleb answered, nodding his head.

Entering the bedroom, He found her curled up on the bed sobbing with her mother sitting next to her.

"Hi, Daisy, how is she?"

"Hi, Brett," Mrs. Anderson replied, shaking her head as she stood up. "She's still upset."

"Rachel honey, I'm so sorry for all this," he apologized, rubbing her back. "You're right, it *is* my fault. I shouldn't have let her go," he continued as Mrs. Anderson left the room.

"No, Brett, it's not your fault," she disagreed, looking up at him with red, swollen eyes. "It's no one's fault. I'm sorry for all I said. I love you."

"I love you too," he replied, taking her in his arms.

"What are we going to do, how are we going to find her?" she asked as his cell phone rang.

"It's the police station, honey!"

"Hello, Mr. Saunders, Detective Smith here, I have some information for you."

"Yes, Detective, go ahead," he answered with a twinge of hope.

"John and Sophia Bennett are not in the Police Database System, which causes me to believe they used *those* names as an alias. Furthermore, we spoke to Daniel Weber, the owner of the building, and presumably they gave him a fake reference."

"Bennett isn't their real name, Detective? And a fake reference?"

"We also found a coffee cup at the bookstore, which is sent to the crime lab to be analyzed for fingerprints."

"That's *some* good news," Brett responded.

"There's an Amber Alert issued for your daughter as well, Mr. Saunders, I'm sorry to tell you this, but I believe Adalyn in a lot of danger. Are you there, Mr. Saunders?" Owen asked as Brett stood silent with the phone to his ear, staring ahead.

"Yes, I'm here, sir," he replied as he came back to reality. "What do we do now?"

"The alert has the phone number posted. Anyone with information can call that number. When the fingerprint results come in, you will need to come down to the station and ID the 'Bennetts' or *whoever* they are."

"How long does that usually take?"

"Forty-eight hours, but I put a rush on it. The forensics team also performed a detailed inspection, and they will give me their report ASAP. You stated earlier that Haley Perkins was Adalyn's friend, is that correct?"

"Yes, she's her best friend. Her mother and father are Logan and Kate Perkins. Their number should be in the telephone directory."

"Okay, I'll check it out and let you know what I find."

"Thanks, Detective."

Chapter 8

Early Tuesday morning at the start of his shift, Owen stood scratching his shaven head, knowing that he needed to investigate all angles concerning the young girl's disappearance. Still awaiting the analysis of the coffee cup, he searched for Haley's phone number. As Adalyn's close friend, she would definitely know something.

"Hello, is this the Perkin's residence?"

"Yes, it is, who am I speaking with?" Kate replied, standing with a dish cloth in her hand.

"Hello, ma'am, this is Detective Smith from the Battleford Police Department. I'm investigating the disappearance of Adalyn Saunders. I understand your daughter and Adalyn are friends?"

"Yes, that's correct, Detective. Haley is heartbroken, she has been crying nonstop. What can I do for you, sir?"

"We need you to come down to the station to answer a few questions?"

"My husband is at work, but I can be there in thirty minutes if that's all right?"

"Yes, and please bring Haley, she may remember something."

"Okay, Detective," Kate replied as she hung up the phone.

"Haley," Kate shouted, "come out here please. We have to go to the police station and answer some questions about Adalyn."

"What kind of questions, mom? I don't know anything."

"I know, baby, but maybe something will jog our memory when the detective is asking the questions."

"I feel awful, Mom, I miss her so much!" She cried as her green eyes glistened with the teardrops.

*****

"Good morning, ladies, come in and have a seat," Owen invited upon their arrival. "This is Detective Lambert here with me."

"Good morning," Kate replied, shaking their hands.

"Haley, you are Adalyn's best friend, correct?" he asked as his deep voice echoed, making Haley nervous.

"Yes, sir, I am," she answered in a shaky tone.

"Can you remember anything different that may have happened with her during the past month?" He smiled a little as to alleviate her jitters.

"No, not that I can think of, sir, we went swimming and hung out. Wait! She said she had met a man at the library. His name was John," she replied confidently, relaxing somewhat.

"Did you ever see him?"

"Yes, one day at the park. He was with a woman, and he smiled at Adalyn while we were leaving. She called me a few days later telling me that she was going to help out at his bookstore."

"I know the man she's talking about," Kate interrupted. "He owns Bennett's bookstore."

"Yes, that's correct," Owen answered.

"Wait! I've seen him somewhere else," Kate continued, "but I can't remember where. Give me a minute, I'll try and remember."

"Haley, can you remember the color of the car?" he asked, turning his focus toward her.

"It was a dark color, black or dark blue."

"Mrs. Perkins, by any chance did you see the license plate number?"

"Detective!" Haley interrupted excitedly. "I remember the license plate number on the car he was driving had the first two initial's *K* and *P*. I noticed it because they are the same as Mom's. I pointed it out to Adalyn at the time."

"Excellent work, Haley," he commended as he wrote the details in his book.

"Oh! And I know where I saw them," Kate shouted. "It was at the hardware store in North Battleford. They were buying two or three rolls of duct tape, acetone, and bleach. I thought it was a weird combination of items since they owned a bookstore."

"That is really good information, ladies, anything else that you can think of?"

"No, that's it."

"Okay, you are free to go, but if you think of anything else, no matter how insignificant you may think, please call me immediately."

"Yes, we will, Detective."

Picking up her purse, Kate took Haley by the hand and walked out the door.

*****

"Sir, doesn't bleach and acetone form chloroform?" Pete asked, requiring confirmation on what he suspected.

"Yes, it does, and chloroform is used to render a person unconscious. Pete! This is not good! That little girl is in trouble! We need the date when they bought the items. Let's go check out the hardware store."

"Right behind you," Pete replied.

*****

Entering the hardware store, they immediately looked for the manager's office to determine the details surrounding the suspicious items bought by the Bennetts.

"Hello, I'm Detective Owen Smith with the Battleford Police Department, and this is Detective Lambert. Are you the manager?"

"Yes, my name is Bradley. What can I do for you, Detective?" he replied as he shook his hand.

"We are investigating a couple who may have purchased some items at this store. Do you have video surveillance?"

"Yes, we do, what time frame are you looking for?" he asked, already beginning his search.

"Give us the last two months."

As Bradley played back each day, both Owen and Pete observed very closely.

"Wait" Pete exclaimed. "Right there," he said, pointing at the screen. "Can you pause and enhance it?"

Buying the items in question were the Bennetts, but unfortunately neither Owen or Pete knew what they looked like.

"What's the date on it?" Owen asked.

"July 28," he replied.

"Two days before Adalyn went missing," Pete observed, looking at Owen.

"Bradley, we are going to need that video footage," Owen insisted as he put his notebook in his front pocket.

"Yes, sir."

"Thank you, you've been a great help. We'll see ourselves out," Owen stated after receiving the video evidence.

*****

Later that evening, Veronica from the police crime lab presented Detective Owen with the results of the coffee cup. Prints were lifted belonging to a man named Lawrence Moore.

Typing the name into the database, Owen examined the profile of a man looking to be in his early to midfifties. Possessing a criminal record, he was arrested for three counts of petty theft and two counts of armed robbery at two different bank locations, resulting in prison time five years ago and nothing on record for him since.

"That's the guy at the hardware store," Pete expressed. "The one we saw on the video surveillance."

It was time to call Brett and Rachel!

"Hi, Mr. Saunders, this is Detective Smith calling. We have the results of the prints on the coffee cup. We need you and your wife to come down to the station to ID the man."

"Yes, we'll be right down," Brett agreed as he turned to Rachel while ending the call.

"I'll call my parents and ask them to watch Caleb while we are gone," he suggested as she went in to get him ready.

*****

Entering the police station, Rachel felt scared even though they were on their way to potentially ID John Bennett. As she walked down the long corridor, she observed several offices. Some were empty, and others were occupied by officers with strained looks on their faces. She assumed they each were attempting to solve some sort of crime. Suddenly, the thought that nothing would improve entered her mind and the feeling of complete loss of Adalyn took over.

"Are you all right, Rachel?" Brett asked as he noticed her eyes squinting as if her entire head was overloaded with despairing thoughts.

"No, I feel a little funny. Maybe it's the fact that we are in a police station ready to identify the man who kidnapped our daughter," she replied with her hand to her forehead.

"I know, honey. Let's hurry and get this over with," he stated as they began to walk faster.

Meeting them in the corridor, Pete escorted them to Owen's office.

"Mr. And Mrs. Saunders, the results of the fingerprints on the cup belong to a man named Lawrence Moore."

"We don't know anyone by that name, Detective," Brett replied, shaking his head.

"We want you to look at his picture to see if you can identify him," Owen stated as he turned the computer screen around to face them.

"That's him," Rachel screamed as her eyes popped, pointing at the screen.

"That's John Bennett, Detective," Brett affirmed in a confident tone.

"John's real name is Lawrence Moore, and he has a criminal record."

"For what?" Rachel asked, grasping a nearby chair to steady herself from the dizziness she was beginning to experience.

"It started with petty theft until it escalated to armed robbery. He served time in prison for it."

"We think he's after money," Pete explained.

"We have no money, Pete, why would they take Adalyn?"

With a lump forming in Owen's throat, he prepared to tell them what the possibility could be. "I'm sorry to have to tell you this," he began, "but we think that their greed for money has escalated and have taken on a whole new meaning since they have kidnapped your daughter. We now may be dealing with a sex trafficker, and they make a lot of money selling young girls."

"What did you just say, Detective?" Rachel yelled as she sat in the chair for fear of falling.

"It's a billion-dollar industry, and young girls are bought and sold every day. This may never be the case for Adalyn, but if it is, I wanted you to be prepared for it."

"Aahh!" Rachel screamed in pain at hearing the news. "Brett, something is wrong! Something is wrong with the baby!" she shouted, holding her stomach.

"We need to go to the hospital right away," Brett exclaimed, helping Rachel to stand.

"I'll drive you," Pete stated as he ran to get his keys.

"Brett, can you call your parents and ask them if Caleb can stay with them for a little while longer?" Rachel managed to say through the pain.

"Yes, I will, on the way to the hospital."

Chapter 9

Bound by duct tape, Adalyn laid helpless on the back seat of yet another vehicle. While unconscious, Seth had exchanged money with John for her. Now with a man she hadn't met before, she would soon detect a violence from him that was worse than John. Regaining consciousness, her world remained dark with the aid of the blindfold and with the smell of sweat emanating from the driver combined with the motion of the vehicle as they hit every bump, she was becoming nauseous. Not on one particular station, the radio produced a low static noise that didn't seem to bother whoever was in the truck.

"Where am I?" She moaned as her head swayed back and forth. "Please, mister, let me go! Let me call my dad, please!" she pleaded.

"Be quiet out there," he yelled as he slammed hard on the brakes to avoid hitting the car in front, causing her to roll off the seat, landing on her stomach.

Grimacing in pain, she pushed herself up to kneeling position, and unable to refrain any longer, she vomited on the floor in front of her.

"Now look what you've done," he scolded, pulling over to the side of the road.

"Momma, I need you," she cried and cried and cried.

Opening the back door, he grabbed her arm, lifting her onto the seat again. The smell was so bad, he had no choice but to clean it up.

"One more word from you and it will be lights out," he promised as he grumbled to himself.

Quieting her sobs to a whimper so as to not anger him, she feared he was a much more enraged version of John. Listening intently to any and all sounds to help identify her surroundings, she was unable to distinguish their location. Unconscious for most of the trip, it was impossible to know how far they had drove.

Having a rancid taste in her mouth from the incident a few minutes before, she chanced to ask him for a drink, unaware of what he would do.

"I told you to keep quiet," he snapped.

"Please, mister, I'm so thirsty."

"NO!" he shouted. "Don't ask again!"

Deciding to obey him, she drifted off to sleep as they drove onward. The destination, she did not know, or what was in store for her.

A tremendous amount of driving hours passed before Seth pulled into an abandoned parking lot. Awakening to the sound of the door opening, she was startled when Seth pulled off the blindfold and cut the duct tape from her hands.

Forcing her out of the truck, she stared at the building in front of her. A large deserted warehouse, with paint virtually non-existent and absent of windows, resided in the middle of nowhere. Standing three feet in height, grass had grown around the building and was clearly neglected. No cars were visible, and she wondered where on earth they were going.

"Where are you taking me?" she asked, trudging through the tall stalks of the meadow.

"Move!" he demanded, pushing her forward.

As he opened the huge steel door of the building, she came face to face with the beginning of what her future held. Before her was a stage-like platform, where she witnessed the parading of young girls. Tables surrounded the stage and consisted of both male and female occupants. As Seth nudged her along, she could hear a *bidding war* for these girls.

"What's goin' on?" she asked as fear arose within her and not really wanting to know the answer.

"Move!" he ordered, grabbing her arm and dragging her toward the stage.

Standing in line, she glanced at the *bidders*. Each table held men dressed in dark suits and women in ritzy dresses. Money was no option, and they were willing to pay for what they wanted.

"No, no, I can't go up there. I can't do it," she screamed upon realizing she was next.

"Now, little girl, you listen to me! I know who your family is and where they live. If you don't cooperate, I will punish *them* and make them pay for each time you don't listen. When they call your name, smile and walk confidently across that stage. You are worth a lot of money, so ensure they keep bidding on you."

He knows everything about me, she thought, horrified, as her face grimaced. *I've been sold into the sex industry, and I have no choice but to protect my family.*

Looking up, she placed her foot on the first step. The five stairs before her appeared to be an insurmountable hill to climb. It was now *her* turn as Seth gave her "information" to one of the men.

With trembling legs, she began to climb but stumbled as her foot missed the third step.

"Go! Get up there!" Seth yelled.

Choking back tears, she stood up and climbed to the top. *How am I going to do this?* she thought. *I can't look a person in the eye, and now I have to march in front of these awful people?* What she didn't know was that walking across that stage was the easy part. Her nightmare was going to be the successful person who bought her.

Forcing herself to smile, she proceeded in a straight line until she heard a male voice telling her to stop. Standing in the middle of the stage, facing the front, she waited as he announced her *qualities*.

"Adalyn is a twelve-year-old Canadian girl. She has fair skin with no rashes or pimples. Her hair is naturally brown, and her eyes are blue. She is pure and undefiled. Let the bidding start!"

"$8000," a man in a black suit began.

"$10,000," yelled a woman.

"$12,000," shouted another woman wearing a red dress.

"$18,000," a man to her right called, holding up his paper.

"$22,000," a man to her left roared, jumping up.

Peering over at Seth, Adalyn could see him grinning from ear to ear at the bidding war going on for her.

"$28,000," shouted one of the women.

Looking up, she watched as the man to her right stood to his feet. "$35,000," he stated in an authoritative voice.

A long pause developed after the last bid as everyone remained silent.

"$35,000, going once," the announcer stated, searching the room. "$35,000, going twice . . . Sold to the gentleman on the right," he announced, pointing his hand toward him.

"Adalyn, you can leave the stage now," he informed her.

Not a single person cared about her crying as she reached the bottom step, or to the fact that her stomach ached because it had been hours since she drank or eaten anything. Grabbing her arm, Seth led her to a room where they exchanged money for her. Now belonging to another stranger, she feared what would come next.

Reluctantly following him out of the building, she noticed a black SUV with a grill-type feature in front, waiting for them. The headlights were striking as they shone a bluish tinged light out into the dusk. As the owner of such an expensive vehicle, he was evidently rich! Rich from girls like her forced to work for him. Before climbing into the back seat, she quickly looked around. The city lights encompassed her, but everything else was unrecognizable.

Driving an hour before stopping again at a gas station, the men allowed her to use the washroom but with supervision. Upon returning to the vehicle, she found a bottle of water and a sandwich waiting for her on the back seat. Gratefully, she ate as swiftly as possible and drank the full bottle of water, unaware of when her next meal would come.

Another hour and forty minutes rapidly passed by, and she cringed as they pulled into a driveway of a normal-looking, large, white, two-story house with black shutters to the windows. It had a burgundy front door and an unattached garage off to the side.

With an elaborate interior, she stood in the foyer and gazed at the tremendous staircase in front of her. Dark brown stained pillars stood on either side to the entrance of what appeared to be a never-ending flight of stairs with an extravagant crystal chandelier hanging from the ceiling in the midst of it.

Consisting of crinkly, auburn hair, a woman appeared from the kitchen and spoke to the men that accompanied Adalyn.

"Is this my latest purchase?" she asked, eyeballing Adalyn. "What's her name?"

"Adalyn is all I know," replied one of the men.

"That's fine, their names are of no concern to my clients."

"Come with me," she demanded. "You need to get ready."

Chapter 10

—◦◦⟨⟩◦◦—

Swerving in and out of heavy traffic that Tuesday evening, Pete escorted Brett and Rachel to the hospital. With sirens blaring, he raced as quickly as possible to get a frightened Rachel to a doctor.

Driving straight to the emergency entrance, he stopped and let Brett out to grab a wheelchair, noticing several ambulances at the same time, and feared the hospital staff were really busy. As he helped Rachel out of the vehicle, she screamed in pain. *They needed to get in there right away*, he thought as Brett came running with the wheelchair.

"My wife needs help," Brett shouted at the receptionist. "She's three months pregnant and in a lot of pain. We've had complications with our other two children. Please hurry."

"Right away, sir. Come with me," she motioned as she led them to an examination room and instructed him to fill out some insurance papers. "A nurse will be with you shortly."

"Brett, the pain is getting worse, we can't lose this baby." She exhaled through pursed lips.

"I know, honey, just hang on, the doctor will be here soon," he stated, rubbing her back, trying to ease her pain.

Lying to her side on the hospital bed, with her knees pulled up to her stomach, she watched as medical personnel hustled through the halls. One emergency after another and now she was one.

"Hi, are you Rachel Saunders?" a nurse asked, walking into their room.

"Yes." She moaned.

70

"My name is Sydney. How are you feeling?"

"The pain is getting worse. I'm afraid for this baby, I've had complications before with my other two pregnancies."

"I'm going to take your vitals and do an ultrasound. I know it's hard, but try and relax," Sydney instructed as she prepared to perform the tasks.

Taking the blood pressure cuff off her arm, Sydney could not hide a look of concern from a frightened Rachel.

"What is it? What's my blood pressure?" she asked with her head propped up, waiting for the answer.

"170/92. What is your normal reading?"

"I think it was around 110/76 the last time I had my checkup," an unsure Rachel replied.

"The doctor will assess that when she sees you. I'm going to give you an ultrasound now. How many weeks are you?"

"Twelve," replied Rachel with misty eyes.

Scanning Rachel's stomach, Sydney could hear the familiar sounds of the baby's heartbeat. "There it is." She smiled. "Can you hear it? Strong beats, 150 per minute, and there's the baby, moving his or her little fingers."

Gazing upon the monitor, Rachel's eyes began to sting as her bottom lids surrendered their oversized teardrops onto her flushed cheekbones. Just the same as Adalyn and Caleb, this baby meant everything to them, and she was thankful he or she was all right.

"Can you describe your pain?" Sydney asked as she wheeled the monitor away from the bed.

"It felt like my stomach was 'cramping,'" she responded, smoothing her stomach.

"What were you doing when it started and how long did they last?"

As her crying grew more intense, she relayed the horrifying details to Sydney. Yesterday morning, they had dropped Adalyn off at the store, and now tonight she was missing.

"Oh, I'm so sorry," Sydney replied. "No wonder your blood pressure is so high. I'll get the doctor right away," she promised, turning away to prevent Rachel from seeing her gently dabbing underneath her eyes from the tears.

"Shhh, I'm here, sweetheart," Brett hushed, putting his arms around her as she wept. "We will find Adalyn, and this baby is going to be all right."

"What are they doing with her, Brett? Where are they taking her? She must be so scared. Our little girl, Brett!" Rachel sobbed, not hearing what he had just said to her.

Interrupting Brett's response was a knock on the door by a medium height, middle-aged woman.

"Hi, I'm Dr. Lily Parsons, with the Obstetrics and Gynecology Department. I was just finishing my shift when I was paged, and I'm glad they caught me. How are you feeling, Mrs. Saunders?"

Dr. Parsons looked on with sympathy as Rachel explained the whole situation.

"I am so sorry," she stated, shaking her head and her eyes full of compassion.

"All we can do is wait for the police. We feel helpless," Brett replied.

"Everything is fine where the baby is concerned as long as the cramping stops," Dr. Parsons began. "I'm going to order bloodwork and admit you for overnight observation. We need to monitor your blood pressure, because the stress you are undergoing probably caused it to spike."

"I'm sorry, Doctor, but we can't stay. We need to look for Adalyn." Rachel sobbed with a tissue to her eyes.

"I know, Mrs. Saunders, but like you said, you can't do anything but wait for the police."

"That's okay, Doctor," Brett replied. "We will stay here. Rachel honey, you need bedrest, this baby is counting on us," he continued as she laid her head back on the pillow.

"Sydney will be right in to help get you settled. You're a little dehydrated as well, Mrs. Saunders, so I've ordered some IV fluids for you.

Nodding again, she tried to smile. It was impossible to do, knowing what her little girl was going through.

"I'll call my parents and tell them what's going on and ask if Caleb can stay the night," Brett stated.

As she laid back on her pillow to try and relax, it was impossible, because her mind was racing with thoughts of the last few days. Just a while ago, they were all together having fun as a family, and now everything was crazy. Contemplating on the preacher's sermon about how God is our provider and protector, she began to reflect back and had to admit that she kept God at a distance. He was indeed good to them and she attended church every Sunday out of *duty*, but that's where He *stayed*, at church. He wasn't a part of her life from Monday to Saturday, but what she failed to realize was that He was waiting to have a relationship with her—with the both of them.

Finally, within fifteen minutes, exhaustion won and she drifted off to sleep.

Returning to the room, Brett looked at his wife as she slept. Her ashen-colored face revealed the stress she was enduring, and even though she was asleep, he could see that she was mentally and physically exhausted.

Placing a blanket over her and about to kiss her on the forehead, he was interrupted by the sound of his cell phone ringing.

"Hi, Mr. Saunders, Detective Smith here, how's your wife?"

"She's resting right now, and the baby is fine," he replied, stepping out into the corridor as to not wake Rachel.

"That's good to hear. I'm calling you to ask if you know the Bennett's home address?"

"Yes, I do, we had a meal with them last week."

"A meal?" Owen asked, surprised as his voice rose a few octaves.

"Yes, Detective, a *meal!* They appeared to be good people, we trusted them. It *seemed* safe to let Adalyn help out at their store."

"What's the address?" He shook his head in disbelief.

After relaying the information, Brett asked him to call if he found anything.

Returning to the room, he sat in the chair next to Rachel's bed, as one thought after another began entering his mind about the possibilities of what was happening to Adalyn. Becoming anxious and worrisome, he jumped up pacing the floor. He tried pushing the thoughts aside but to no avail, they kept invading his mind. Leaving the room again, as to escape Rachel from seeing him like that, he paced the halls instead. Adalyn was so precious to him, and he was beside himself at the thought of someone hurting her.

Chapter 11

A dalyn stood shaking in Tessa's kitchen, the woman who paid $35,000 for her. Questions swirled in her head. What did she want from her? Why did she need to get ready? Where was she going? These people had a lot of money, and they meant business.

"Come with me," Tessa ordered.

"Where am I going?" Adalyn asked, following her up the stairs.

"You need to be ready for Eric. Paige will give you a dress to wear and do your makeup. I have to 'pretty' up the *package* before I can sell it," she sneered.

"Eric? I don't understand, ma'am."

"Child, do you know what's happening to you?" she asked as she kept climbing the stairs, not facing Adalyn.

"I think I do, but I'm confused," she answered in a brittle voice ready to cry.

"You are going to be a 'special' little girl to a very wealthy man. You are worth a lot of money in your condition."

"Condition?" Adalyn asked, peering up at the lady.

"Yes, you haven't been with a man before, correct?"

"A man?" Adalyn felt the room spin as it became dark before collapsing onto the floor.

Annoyed, Tessa knelt down beside her. "Wake up!" she shouted, smacking her on the cheek.

Blinking, Adalyn's eyes began to focus, and she witnessed a disgruntled slit-eyed Tessa frowning down on her. Her head throbbed, and she was still woozy from all she had endured over the past couple of days, but this woman had no sympathy. "Get up!" she ordered. "You are wasting precious time."

A different lady stood in one of the other bedrooms and motioned for her to come in.

"Please tell me what is happening to me?" Adalyn pleaded, sitting on a chair next to her.

"Tessa bought you from an auction, and now you belong to her. She will sell you again to a very rich man named Eric, and you will be *his* girl alone until he grows tired of you. Marked as damaged goods by then, he will sell you to a brothel house where you will live for a long time."

"A brothel?" Adalyn questioned. "What is a brothel?"

Adalyn stared at her with disbelief as Paige described the house that she would be sold to. *Is this a nightmare?* she thought. *Is this really happening to me?*

Finishing her makeup, Paige instructed her to get dressed. Leaving the room in a daze, Adalyn walked to yet another bedroom to find a red dress waiting for her.

"I'm not wearing that," she yelled. "What's wrong with my own clothes?"

Walking by, Tessa heard Adalyn as she spoke the words. "Listen to me," she demanded, grabbing her hair, "you are my property, and you will obey my orders. You will put on that dress and be downstairs in ten minutes! Understand?"

"No! I won't do it!" she screamed in a shrill and childlike manner. "I'm not going with any man, you can't make me."

"If you're not going to do this the easy way, you will spend the night locked up out in my garage."

"What?" Adalyn gasped.

"You heard me," she roared. "Let's go!" Grabbing her by the arm, Tessa dragged her down the stairs and all the way out to the garage. As she opened the door, Adalyn could see a large crate with a lock and key toward the left wall. Empty paint cans cluttered the corner to her far right, while numerous piled boxes occupied the other. Sitting on a bench next to the right wall were pieces of board in varying lengths, and broken plumbing supplies were deposited all over the garage floor. A lawnmower and several gardening tools were thrown around wherever they could find a place, and the stench of garbage bags told her, they were present. It was a very disheveled area, the complete opposite of her grandiose house.

"Get in there," Tessa ordered as she opened the crate and shoved her inside.

"No! You can't leave me here," Adalyn's voice quavered under the strain of being left there overnight. "Please, lady, please, I can't stay here, I'm afraid of the dark. Please don't leave me here!" Her cries went unheard to an unaffected Tessa.

"I will return tomorrow morning for you. Be ready to obey me," she threatened. As Adalyn watched her leave through the openings of the crate, she heard Tessa's cell phone ring.

"Yes, hello, Eric."

"Is that little package ready for pick up yet?" he asked as his loud and unpleasant voice echoed in her ear.

"No, Eric, not quite, she will be ready tomorrow morning."

"I'm sorry to hear that, Tessa. I expected more from you, I am extremely disappointed."

"She's not ready to cooperate yet. She needs to be 'conditioned,'" Tessa explained.

"Conditioned?" he asked. "Do you mean punish her by any means until she complies to our rules?"

"Yes, that's exactly what I'm talking about. She will have a change of heart tomorrow."

"I may go elsewhere for what I need," he said. "Tomorrow is a long time away."

"As you wish, Eric. She's a sure deal, and I have men lined up for a girl like her that will pay above asking price. I will not have trouble selling her."

"I'll wait until 8:00 tomorrow morning, not a moment after."

"You have a deal, see you then."

Adalyn cried until the tears ceased to flow. *Why is this happening to me?* she asked herself. *I'm a good girl, from a great family, and I'm an excellent student. Why?*

Hearing every creaking sound, she sat in the darkness stiff and trembling with fright. Her momma had always left a night light on for her when she slept; and now she was facing one of her biggest fears alone, without anyone next to her. With her head resting on her knees, she realized that due to the size of the crate, she would have to remain in that position for the rest of the night.

Beginning to doze off, she became suddenly alert to the sound of tiny footsteps scurrying across the floor. Her body froze as she heard it run close to the crate. "What's that?" she cried out. It was too dark to see. "Please go away! Please go away!" She begged as her eyes scrunched with fright.

"Daddy, I need you." She sobbed. "I'm afraid, it's so dark here. I can't move my legs, it hurts too much." As she tried shifting her position, she was defeated by the four sides of the crate, but she no longer heard the tiny sounds of the critter. As her eyes began to close from exhaustion, she slept periodically throughout the night.

Daylight finally began to break at five thirty. Breathing a sigh of relief, she knew the night was over, but with the daylight, came Tessa. Soon to be coming for her, Tessa would sell her to Eric, a man she didn't know. A man who would become her first encounter, an encounter that a twelve-year-old should never have to endure.

Opening the garage door at seven in the morning, Tessa appeared. "Hurry and stand to your feet," she ordered as she unlocked the crate. "Eric is coming for you at eight, and you need to be ready. Take a shower, put on the dress I've laid out for you, and meet me in the kitchen."

Following her into the house, Adalyn obeyed her every command for fear of a repeat of last night.

As she made her appearance in the kitchen, she found two slices of plain bread and a glass of water on the counter. "Go ahead, eat." Tessa glared. "Eric will be here soon."

Wiping away her tears, she ate quickly as she remembered her momma's homemade bread and how fresh and delicious it was. *Will I ever taste it again?* she asked herself.

"Come here," Tessa demanded, interrupting her thoughts. "Eric is here for you."

Walking out into the foyer, she looked up at the tall man waiting for her. He appeared to be sixty years old with gray hair. She assumed he was wealthy from the expensive black suit and black shoes he wore. The ring on his right hand told her that he had graduated from a powerful university.

"You were right, Tessa," he sneered, "she's a *looker*!"

"We can take care of the payment in my office," Tessa motioned.

"Seventy grand is my price," she said with confidence.

"Tessa!" Eric grunted. "She's not worth that kind of money!"

"Oh, but she is," Tessa argued. "In fact, she's worth more. A twelve-year-old white girl that has never been touched? Oh yes, seventy thousand dollars and not a penny less. I have a list of clients waiting to pay that much for her. You can pay up or you can stop wasting my time."

With an envelope full of money, he used it to buy Adalyn as Tessa gave him all her family information as collateral to use against her in times of disobedience.

As they exited the house and into his SUV, she had no idea where they were going. Sitting in the back seat trembling with what was about to happen to her, she spoke not a word but began thinking of her parents and her best friend, Haley, and how she missed them so.

Chapter 12

Early Wednesday morning, Owen arrived at his office thirty minutes before his shift. The Saunders' case had kept him awake all night going over the facts. As he was sitting at his desk, he received a call from the forensics team in North Battleford.

"Good morning, Detective, this is Dex from forensics. I'm calling to let you know that a thorough search was conducted of the bookstore and its perimeter. A rag was found twenty feet away from the store and is now gone to the forensics lab for testing. The results will be in later today."

"Thanks, Dex. Call me as soon as you get them."

*****

"As Owen and Pete sat eating lunch in the local restaurant, Dex called back with the results."

"Detective, the rag tested positive for acetone and sodium hypochlorite."

"Hmm!" Owen pondered. "Sodium hypochlorite is also known as your common household bleach, am I correct?"

"Yes, that's right," Dex replied.

"I guess we have the item that was used to put Adalyn to sleep. Thanks, Dex."

"What is it, sir?" Pete questioned as he ate a bite of his sandwich.

"The rag tested for acetone and bleach, which as we know forms Chloroform."

"That's what they used for Adalyn," Pete stated pushing his plate away, suddenly losing his appetite.

"We have to get back to the station and call the Saunders," Owen said as he jumped up throwing two twenty-dollar bills on the table to pay for their lunch. "We also need to search the Bennett's home."

*****

Back at the station, Owen instructed Pete to call Brett while he was calling for another search warrant for the Bennett's home.

"Hi, Brett, it's Pete calling."

"Do you have any more leads, Pete?" he asked as his voice rose in anticipation for good news.

"Yeah, I'm sorry, Brett, but a rag was found twenty feet from the store. It tested positive for two substances. Those substances when combined form chloroform."

"Chloroform puts you to sleep, right?" he questioned as his voice returned to its former hopelessness with thoughts of things getting worse instead of improving.

"Yes, it does. The bad part about all this is that Lawrence a.k.a. John and Sophia had bought those items plus duct tape two days prior to Adalyn's disappearance."

"Are you saying that's what they used to put her to sleep?" Brett yelled from despondency.

"We're not entirely certain, but it looks that way."

"No, Pete! That's my little girl," he shouted. "What are they doing to her?"

"I know, Brett. We are doing everything we can to find her. Continue taking care of Rachel, Caleb, and the baby. We'll do our part on this end, and God will do the rest."

"Thanks, Pete," he replied, hanging up the phone as he tumbled onto the chair so discouraged and downhearted.

Although Brett was doing his best to stay strong for everyone, Pete could hear the heaviness in his voice and this was affecting Brett more than he realized.

Meanwhile, Owen made the call to Kari Rhodes for another warrant.

"Hello, Ms. Rhodes, Detective Smith here."

"Yes, Detective, what can I do for you?"

"I need another search warrant for the Adalyn Saunders case."

"For where?"

"To search the Bennett's home."

"What evidence do you have to support it, Detective?" she asked.

"John Bennett used an alias. His correct name is Lawrence Moore. A rag was found twenty feet from the bookstore, which tested positive for acetone and bleach. We have video surveillance of him and his female partner buying those items along with duct tape at a hardware store in North Battleford. He has a criminal record, Ms. Rhodes!"

"I'll make an appeal to Judge Watkins right away," Kari replied

As Owen waited for the warrant, he called North Battleford, and requested a forensics team to help with the search of the Bennett's home.

With everything in place, Owen, Pete, and the team headed for their destination.

Upon entering the house, Owen observed how well they had cleaned it. The appliances were the only things left.

"Look for anything and everything," Owen instructed, "they must have missed *something* here."

Both unsuccessful as they searched the house, they presumed the kidnapping was well-planned. With nothing left behind, Owen performed once last search of the living area as Pete headed for the kitchen.

"Hey, boss! Out here! I think I may have something," Pete yelled out while down on his knees closely examining an area on the floor.

"Where?" Owen asked, running out into the kitchen.

"Here under the refrigerator! It looks like a small sliver of glass!"

Upon inspection, Owen realized Pete was right.

"Great find, Pete, bag it and send it off with forensics and tell them to put a rush on it because time is running out for Adalyn. Her life is depending on us. Take my car and I'll hitch a ride back to the precinct with one of the other officers."

"I'm on it, sir," Pete replied as he hurried out the door.

"Hey, guys," Owen shouted, "can you test for blood around the refrigerator?"

"Yes, we can," Dex answered as he walked over. "Luminol will give us the answers we are looking for."

As they conducted the procedure, they found there was indeed blood on the floor and someone had attempted to get rid of the evidence.

"From the small amount of blood found," Dex informed Owen, "it appears the person may have encountered a laceration and then cleaned up the spillage."

"That may explain the small piece of glass we just found," Owen replied. "Hopefully we will find some DNA."

Chapter 13

———◦◦◦———

D
r. Parsons had ordered Rachel an overnight stay in the hospital for some needed bedrest and observation. Although spending the night there, sleep was not readily available. Tossing and turning with thoughts of Adalyn, it kept her from obtaining the rest she needed. As she twisted to her left, she questioned, *Where is she? What are they doing to her?* Rolling to her right, she pictured Adalyn in the hands of very wicked people. It was impossible to expect her to relax.

In a chair next to her bed, Brett sat dozing in and out of sleep. With his head laid back and one leg up over the arm, he too spent a disturbed night. Opening her eyes, Rachel could see the cell phone still in his hand from the call Pete had made to him just after lunch, informing him of what the police had discovered.

"ADALYN!" he screamed as he jumped from his chair, looking around the hospital room. Turning to see a wide-eyed Rachel staring at him, he suddenly remembered where they were and the nightmare he had woke up from was a stark reality.

"Rachel, she's gone." He sobbed clinging to her. "She's really gone! My baby girl, what are they doing to her?" he continued as she embraced him.

"Brett, have you received any calls from Detective Owen with new information?" she asked through the tears.

Standing up, he began walking around the room agonizing whether to tell her what he knew. The information would definitely upset her, and he feared it would put added stress on their unborn baby. He decided to chance in telling her and hoped he could keep her calm somehow.

"Yes, honey, Pete called to let us know what they had discovered."

"Is it good news?" she asked, expecting a positive answer, but knowing if it was, he would have told her by now.

"No, I'm sorry, Rachel, it's not good news. But you have to promise me that you will try to stay calm when I tell you. Think about our unborn baby."

"Brett, you're scaring me, just tell me."

"The police have video surveillance of Lawrence a.k.a. John and his girlfriend buying suspicious items at the hardware store in North Battleford, two days prior to Adalyn's disappearance."

"What kind of items?"

"Duct tape, acetone, and bleach," he reluctantly replied, studying her facial reactions for signs of stress.

"Yes okay, but why the concern with *those* things?" she asked. "WAIT! Are you saying they used duct tape to restrain her?" she screamed

"Rachel, please calm down. We don't know that for sure."

"Well, it sure appears that way," she argued. "What about the other things? The bleach and stuff. What are they for?" she asked with an angry tone.

"Rachel, that's all I'm going to say. It's putting too much stress on you and the baby."

"OH NO, Brett! You have to tell me, I need to know or I will think the worst." She glared at him with penetrating eyes as if this was all his fault.

Nothing was as worse as this, he thought. "Those two ingredients when mixed together form chloroform, a substance used to . . ."

"Put someone to sleep," she yelled, finishing his sentence. "No! No! No! Brett, I can't bear it! She's so scared, I know it. Brett, we have to find her. Think Brett, how are we going to do it?" She wailed as he sat next to her.

"Rachel, please try and stay calm, I've gone over it in my mind a thousand times, and I can't figure it out. Detective Smith is working around the clock on this, please give him time to do his job. I know you're scared for her and I am too, but we have no idea where they have taken her.

Ready to unleash her frustrations onto him, she decided against it and kept them to herself. He was just as worried as she was and didn't deserve her outbursts.

"Can I get you a drink or something?" he asked, standing to his feet.

"The only thing I want, Brett, is to have Adalyn back!" She sobbed into her pillow.

"I know," he replied. "Me too. I'm going to call my parents and check on Caleb," he said as he left the room, not knowing what else to do for her.

*****

Turning in bed to her side, she began thinking about the whole situation. Question after question bombarded her mind: What was their next move? What would they do when they returned home? Do they wait by the phone for the police to call? She's so young and innocent, how could they hurt her like that? As her breathing began to intensify, her heart rate began to climb, and with shaking hands, she jumped out of bed and attempted to dress. "I have to get out of here," she screamed.

Upon hearing her, a nurse came running to the room. "Mrs. Saunders, are you okay? Where are you going?"

"Adalyn is waiting for me, I have to go," she answered. "Her father and I need to search for her, she's counting on us," she continued, panic-stricken as she rummaged throughout the room looking for her belongings.

"Mrs. Saunders, I understand, but the doctor has to see you first. I will wait with you until your husband returns."

"There's no time, I have to go now, please get out of my way," she ordered.

"Please, ma'am, you're too upset to leave right now, wait until your husband comes to help you."

As she finished putting on her jacket, the nurse called for help as Brett came running down the corridor. "What's wrong?" he asked

"Your wife is really upset and insisting on leaving immediately. She is too distressed to hear our medical advice, so maybe you can reason with her."

Entering the room, he found Rachel in a frenzy, pacing the floor and pushing the IV pole with her. "We're coming, baby," she mumbled. "Hold on, Daddy and I are coming to get you."

"Rachel, what are you doing? Where are you going?" he asked, in a soothing voice, trying to diffuse the situation.

"There you are, Brett," she answered. "We need to go right now and bring our daughter home."

"Rachel sweetheart, listen to me, the police are out looking for her. We have no idea where she is, but Pete is doing all he can to find her."

"No, I cannot wait for them!" she yelled. Adalyn is counting on us, Brett. We are leaving right now!"

"Okay, but first, could you wait for the doctor to examine you? Our new baby need us too."

"There's no time," she screamed, beginning to cry. "Don't you care, Brett?"

At that precise moment, an abundance of compassion swept over him, for her, upon seeing the hurt and desperation in her eyes. Taking her into his arms as she tried to push him away, he knew exactly what she was feeling and why.

"Shhh, we are going to find her," he promised.

Crying for the next ten minutes, she finally relaxed in his arms, but felt hopeless.

As Dr. Parsons walked into the room, she witnessed a very emotional Rachel. With concern, she examined her but was not pleased with the results.

"I'm not going to lie to you, Rachel," she stated. "I know you're upset over losing your daughter, and I would be too, believe me! But the stress is too much for your other child. You need to try and stay calm to help regulate your blood pressure. I've already ordered bedrest, and I cannot send you home unless you give me your word that you will follow my orders and stay in bed until everything is under control."

"Yes okay," Rachel promised. "I will stay on bedrest."

"I will do up the discharge papers, and you can go home," Dr. Parsons stated.

As she was wheeled out, Rachel apologized to the nurse for her behavior.

"That's okay, Mrs. Saunders, I can't imagine what you are going through, I pray you find your little girl and that this little one is safe."

"Thank you for all your help." Rachel smiled as she held the nurse's hand.

*****

With Rachel situated in bed, Brett drove to his parents to bring Caleb home. He thought of what he would say to his son about what was happening, but nothing good came to mind.

"Come in, son," his father invited. "How's Rachel and the baby?"

"They're both fine right now, but she needs to stay on bedrest for a while and definitely has to try and stay calm, or we will lose the baby."

"I'm so sorry, Brett," his mother sympathized as she walked into the kitchen. "Do you have any more news on Adalyn?"

"Some information has come to light, but we are not any closer to finding her," he replied as he broke down crying, rubbing his eyes and forehead.

"Don't lose hope, Brett, they'll find her."

"Where's Caleb?" he asked in between sobs.

"In the bedroom, I'll call him out," his father said.

Running out, Caleb stopped suddenly at the sight of his dad crying.

"What's wrong, Dad? Is Adalyn back yet? Where's Mom?"

"Mom is at home now, resting, and Adalyn isn't home yet son, we're doing all we can to find her."

"What's going to happen to her, Dad? What if we don't find her?" he kept asking questions as his bottom lip began to tremble.

"We will find her, Caleb, we can't give up hope. Let's go home and see Mom, she misses you," he replied, handing him his sneakers.

"Thanks, Mom and Dad, for all your help," he shouted as he left the house." I'll call when I find out anything more."

*****

"Mom, where are you?" Caleb shouted as he entered the house.

"I'm in the bedroom, honey."

"I missed you, guys," he said as he ran and jumped on the bed next to her.

"We missed you too. I'm so glad to see you." She smiled, giving him a big hug. "How was your stay at Grandma's?" she asked, trying to create some normalcy for him.

"I love it at their house, but I couldn't stop thinking about you and Adalyn," he admitted with saddened eyes.

"I know, but we have to stay strong and keep hoping that we find her," she told him as she hugged him close, not taking for granted any time spent with him.

Chapter 14

—⟨∘⟨⟆⟩∘⟩—

S itting in the back seat of Eric's SUV, Adalyn cried silently to stop him from hearing her as she began thinking about the drive to the library she and her dad made the first time she had met John Bennett. Her memories made her recall the *"don't worry"* comment she had said to her father regarding John, because he was a *"nice"* man. Now on the way to Eric's house, she was about to endure something so difficult that she couldn't even imagine. Thinking of what the outcome would be once they arrived, she became short of breath and found it hard to breathe. Clutching her throat trying to get a deep breath, her cheeks flushed as the blood pooled to that area and her heart raced as she began pulling on the door handle.

"The doors are locked." Eric smirked. "You cannot escape."

"LET ME OUT!" she yelled, continuously yanking on the handle. "I can't get my breath!"

"Yes, you can!" He mocked. "You're having a panic attack! Now sit back and be quiet!"

Taking deeper breaths, she tried to slow her breathing as to calm herself down. He was right, the doors were locked and there was nowhere to run.

*****

Upon arriving at his residence, she surveyed the premises. Refusing to give up the idea of escape, she captured a mental image of his property to help police in his arrest. The dark gray two-story house consisted of a black door and an attached two-car garage. Four brick pillars with a white veranda separating each section stood firm as giants proclaiming *power* and *dominance*, indicative of their owner. The lush garden portrayed perfectly groomed trees and shrubs as well as the lawn with its neatly manicured condition. Eric obviously took pride in his property but lacked *as much* in his character. *How could someone treat their garden with more respect than a human being?* she thought.

Fear shook her entire being with the knowledge of what was awaiting her as she watched the garage door open. Grabbing her arm, he forced her from the vehicle and into the house. Not willing to go without a fight, she began resisting.

"Let me go!" she screamed, kicking him as he dragged her up a flight of stairs and into the master bedroom. As she pounded him with her fists, he began to snarl and shake his head at her resistance, then decided to take her to the bathroom.

"What are you doing?" she asked, ending her boxing match as he turned the tap for the hot water. Ignoring her question, he forced her arm underneath the extremely hot water and kept it there for several minutes as she screeched, causing a first-degree burn.

"That burn is a trademark proving you belong to *me* now." He growled. "It's the first of *many* if you refuse to cooperate." Taking her by the arm once more, he led her downstairs and all the way to the basement. "Get in there," he demanded, pushing her into a small closet. "You will learn the hard way," he muttered as he locked the door.

Barely catching her breath from crying so hard, she slumped onto the floor. Enveloped in darkness yet again, she tried soothing the burn with her tears, only causing it to sting more. As her eyes adjusted to the dark, combined with a glimmer of light from beneath the door, she was able to inspect the tiny space. She imagined it was used for storage as she strained to see a shelf holding two boxes and a pair of shoes; but now it was a place to keep her locked up for causing a disturbance.

Sitting on the floor weeping, she began thinking of her family and how much they were missed. *How will they find me?* she wondered. Unconscious for most of the travelling, the city's name was a mystery to her. Tossed from person to person, vehicle to vehicle, she was well-*hidden* from the world. These people were clever and knew all her intimate details. Attempting to withstand the pain from her burn, she reflected back to a family camping trip. Sitting around enjoying a campfire, she accidently dabbed the calf of her leg on the hot fire poker. Running to her rescue upon hearing the scream, her mom applied cream and a bandage. The pain subsided, and once again her mom was the hero. "Momma, I need you now more than ever." She cried as she lay on the floor drifting off to sleep.

After three hours, she was awakened to the sound of Eric unlocking the room door. "Stand up," he yelled, grabbing her and leading her up the two flights of stairs. "It's *time!*"

"Time for what?" she asked, looking up at him, in hope he would show some compassion.

"Wait for me in the bedroom." He growled.

To avoid punishment, she obeyed his command and walked into the bedroom. "He is never coming near me," she declared, striving to unravel an escape route. Her eyes navigated to a half-opened window and upon inspection, discovered that if she climbed out onto the roof, she could somehow reach the porch below. Opening the window to full height, she lifted one leg out followed by her head and shoulders. *I'm almost there*, she thought excitedly, ready to raise her other leg, but with the attempt came failure as Eric grabbed her foot and snatched her back in.

"Where do you think *you're* going?" he yelled. "Get back in here, I paid top dollar for you, and I plan to have my money's worth."

"No!" She wailed. "Get away from me! Leave me alone!" Disregarding her protests, he threw her onto the bed and was about to join her when she jumped up and headed for the door.

Quickly springing into action, he ran after her, clenching her hair and bringing her to an abrupt stop. "You are a defiant little girl," he complained, striking her with the back of his hand sending her across the floor. Walking toward her, he then kicked hard into her stomach as she screamed in pain. With no sympathy, he continued beating her until her cries dulled to a whimper. Lifting her to her feet, he dragged her down over the stairs again and into the small closet. "You can stay there until I return for you," he ordered. "That attitude of yours *will* be adjusted when I see you again."

Grateful to be back in the room again and away from that awful man, she sat on the floor finding it difficult to breathe. Fearing her ribs were broken from the beating, she curled up in an attempt to maintain a position that would ease the pain. Her whole body ached as she found it too unbearable to cry. Lying motionless on the floor, she dreaded the time when he would return for her.

With his *"possession"* safely locked in the basement, Eric headed out to visit an acquaintance, planning to buy a substance to subdue Adalyn. He was absent for two hours giving her body a chance to rest, but she desperately needed medical attention in which she would not receive from him *or* a doctor. Her thoughts went back to the time where Caleb had broken his ankle playing sports in school. Although she was in excruciating pain, she could somewhat relate to what *he* had felt. She suddenly became *sorry* for not understanding at the time and for feeling a little jealous over the attention he was receiving from everyone. She longed for her dad to pick her up and carry her to the hospital to obtain the care she needed.

Hearing his footsteps coming down the stairs, she shuttered with the thought of him opening the door. With the sound of the key entering the lock, she began trembling with fear from the anticipation of *him*. He was cruel, dangerous, and without a conscience. The idea of spending another minute with him weakened her, but she didn't have a choice.

"Get up!" he roared as the basement light filled the closet.

"Please, mister, I think my ribs are broken," she begged for any kind of sympathy from him.

"I don't care!" he snapped. "Rise to your feet, I will not say it again!"

Grunting from impatience, he watched as she tried her best to stand, and grabbing her hair, he moved her upstairs. "Hold still," he ordered, shoving her into a chair.

"What's that?" she questioned, eyeing the needle in his hand.

"This will make you unable to fight me." He grinned.

Feeling the room spin after he administered the substance, she no longer felt pain from her previous injuries. Scooping her up in his arms, Eric took her to the bedroom. *This* time there would be no fighting. Her little limp body was now going to be *his*.

Chapter 15

—◦◦◦—

Early the next morning, Adalyn laid sleeping in an unfamiliar bed. Opening her eyes, she failed to recognize her surroundings. Still confused from the effects of the night before she looked around trying desperately to remember, but within a few minutes, flashbacks came rushing to her mind. Horrified with what had transpired, she prevented herself from crying too much due to the pain of her broken ribs. The smell of his cologne on her skin made her nauseous, but with an empty stomach, the dry heaves caused her body to ache from the trauma it had endured. As she rubbed her head from the pounding headache she was experiencing, her eyes glanced down at the dark bruising on her legs. Attempting to move, she realized she was chained to the bedpost and unable to wiggle free. She laid on her side as two big tears trickled down each cheek. Feeling dirty and degraded, she felt as though her skin was crawling. She needed a shower to wash the *filth* away; but *that* wasn't going to happen. Now sensing the urge for the bathroom, she pondered her plan of action. Calling for *him* meant *facing* him and then trouble and agony would follow suit.

"Hello, mister! Mister, I need to go to the bathroom," she yelled, not having a choice. "Hello, can you hear me?"

"What do you want?" he barked, walking into the bedroom.

"I need to go to the bathroom," she pleaded as her face strained from torment.

"Wait a minute," he snapped, unlocking the chain.

Slowly crawling out of bed, she began the difficult walk across the floor to the bathroom. With each step she moaned in pain, and the five-second walk seemed to take forever. After closing the door, Eric could hear her scream with anguish, but he felt no sympathy. His only emotion was annoyance. With a hardened heart, he showed no remorse.

Running the tap water for several minutes and flushing the toilet twice in an effort to stall as long as possible, she remained in the bathroom in hope that he would have departed the room.

"Get out here now!" he shouted, waiting for her return.

With her head lowered and her body slumped over, she cringed at the sound of his voice. As she reluctantly opened the door, he grabbed her arm, taking her to the bed and pushed her onto it.

Her cries of distress fazed him not. Jumping on the bed next to her, she struggled to be free, but his overpowering strength pinned her down. Knowing this was a repeat of the night before, she became aware that *this* time, she was well-alert for the entire episode. Deafened by the disgusting sounds coming from him, she pleaded and cried for help. He paid no attention, and no one could hear her. Fearing he was planning to keep her for a long time, she grasped the idea that she was his prisoner *and* she was helpless.

Her limp little body remained still on the bed as he finished with her. Continuously crying, her heart called out for her mom. If only she knew what was happening to her little girl. Imagining her mother's arms around her, stroking her hair, helped her cope with the devastating acts of cruelty that was committed against her.

"Get up!" he ordered. "Come with me!"

Pushing her down the stairs, she stumbled on the last step falling face first onto the floor, busting open her lip. As the blood gushed out, he threw a towel at her and hustled her into the closet. Relieved to be in her *room* again, she was thankful for the solitude as his footsteps disappeared over the top step. Nursing her lip, she dabbed the towel ever so gently to stop the bleeding. With her mouth and tongue dry from thirst, she longed for a glass of water. Her last meal was at Tessa's twenty-six hours ago. Thinking back to an incident where Caleb and herself had argued over the last glass of milk, she sighed at such silly things in light of what she was lacking now. Wondering if he would allow her to eat once he returned, she quickly dismissed the thought for she would rather bear her hunger than see *him* again.

Returning home again after two hours, Adalyn could hear him walking around upstairs. Absent from her for short periods of time, she speculated on how he earned a living and assumed he was retired from a very wealthy income. Wishing he had a job to go to, her eyes closed in despair at the sound of his footsteps nearing the door.

"Get up!" he demanded. "It's time."

"No." She wailed. "Please, mister, can I have some food?"

Frowning, he thought back, trying to remember if he had given her any. A day and a half, she was with him, and he hadn't bothered to give her as much as a glass of water. He realized that if he wanted to keep her, he needed to allow her to eat.

She guzzled down ten plain crackers and gulped a full glass of water before she looked up again. Leading her to the bedroom, she was powerless against him. He made her sick as he had his way again.

Chapter 16

⊃∘C∽∾∘⊂

S itting at his desk early Thursday morning, Detective Smith rubbed his head in frustration. Adalyn had been reported missing since Monday. The abductor and the *means* of the abduction were identified along with the make and model of the car, but where was she? In his thirty-eight-year career, he could understand it if a crime like kidnapping had occurred in the big city of *North Battleford*, but not in a town like Battleford with a population of little more than four thousand people.

What will be my next move? he asked himself. He needed the results from the sliver of glass Pete had found at the Bennett's home. Just as he was thinking about it, his phone rang delivering the results.

"Good morning, Detective, this is Dex from the forensics lab in North Battleford. I have the results of the piece of glass you submitted."

"Good. What did you find?"

"DNA tested positive for Ivy Stratton."

"Ivy Stratton?" Owen asked, puzzled. "Thanks, Dex. Send that report to me ASAP."

Typing the name into the database, it produced the same description as Sophia Bennett with a profile that left Owen speechless.

At the age of twenty, Ivy Stratton served eighteen months in prison for possession of drugs with the intent to sell. Arrested again at twenty-eight years of age, she served ten years for attempted robbery and two accounts of assault against a convenience store employee and a customer. Changing her name, she moved to another province, but trouble quickly followed as she was tried for manslaughter of her boyfriend but was acquitted for insufficient evidence.

Using a second alias to escape her shady past, she fled to yet another province working as a waitress at a small-town diner. Becoming a model employee with hopes of turning her life around looked promising but was crushed when the lure of *big money* plagued her mind. Bragging often to her co-workers about landing a gig with a huge payout, she attempted to kidnap a neighbor's daughter. As the mother fought her, Ivy fled the scene without the daughter and has been on the run ever since. An APB is issued for her arrest.

Oh no! Owen thought, shaking his head. "This CANNOT be the woman who has Adalyn. Pete, get in here now!" he shouted.

"What is it?" Pete asked, running to his office.

"The results are in from the piece of glass that was sent to forensics. The DNA is positive for a woman named Ivy Stratton, and her profile is here on the database."

"Do we know who this woman is?" Pete asked as he finished reading the report.

"Call Brett Saunders and ask him to come down to the station. He may be able to identify her."

"You don't think she is Sophia Bennett, sir, do you?" Pete questioned, rubbing his forehead.

"I don't know, Pete," he replied, grief-stricken. "If it is, then it's going to be a very dangerous situation."

*****

Brett arrived at the station thirty minutes later and headed for Owen's office.

"Come in, Mr. Saunders, and have a seat," Owen instructed. "How is your wife?"

"She's on bedrest until she and the baby are out of danger. It is difficult to keep her blood pressure at a safe level due to all this stress."

"I understand," Owen nodded. "I'm sorry you have to go through all this."

"I am too," Brett replied. "Can you tell me why I'm here, Detective?" he asked as he sat in a chair.

"DNA found at the Bennett's home has produced the results of a woman by the name of Ivy Stratton. Do you recognize this woman?" he asked as he turned the computer screen toward Brett. Pete watched the color escaped from his face as he looked at the picture.

"That's Sophia Bennett!" he said confidently, staring at Owen.

"Are you positive?" Pete asked.

"Yes! Very positive! She is a little younger here in this picture, but that is definitely Sophia! Who did *you* say it was, Detective?"

"Ivy Stratton! She is a wanted criminal, and according to the report, she had attempted to kidnap a little girl *and* she has a vicious temper!"

"WAIT! Hold on for a moment! Are you saying what I think you're saying, Detective? This woman has Adalyn? Don't tell me that, Pete!" he yelled, jumping out of his chair. "My poor Addy! My little girl! How can I tell Rachel this?" he exclaimed. "How, Detective? How do I tell her these savages have our daughter?"

"Wait, Brett! Calm down! We are not a hundred percent sure of what you are thinking," Owen replied as he stood as well.

"Come on, Detective! *You know!* It's written all over your faces! This woman fits the profile of someone who would take Adalyn. So tell me the truth! What do you think?"

"I'm sorry, Brett, I cannot make a comment until we get concrete evidence to prove it."

Covering his eyes with his hand, Brett began weeping. "What are we going to do?" He cried as he fell into a nearby chair. "How are we going to find her?"

"Brett, I have three children and grandchildren," Owen sympathized. "I can only imagine what you are going through."

Pete looked at Owen as he sensed that Brett needed something more than sympathy. "Detective?" he began to ask, "Brett is a friend of mine, would it be okay if I took him into the other room and spoke to him for a few minutes?"

"You can talk to him here in my office," Owen nodded. "I'll grab a coffee, take all the time you need," he continued as he left the room.

Watching him cry in despair and unsure of what to say, Pete took a deep breath. "Never give up hope, Brett. We will do our absolute best to find her."

"Pete! Do you understand what I am going through?" he shouted with both hands in the air. "Two criminals kidnapped my little girl and have possibly sold her into *that* industry! THAT industry!" he repeated. "I can't even say the word. Just the thought of it sickens me. What are they doing to her?"

"Okay, Brett! I *need* to say this to you, not as a cop but as a friend. I believe this is a very serious situation, one in which we need God to step in. I know how you feel about it, but I'm telling you, God *can* bring her back home to you."

"Pete, I believe God is up there somewhere, but He doesn't have a part in my life like He does yours. How can I ask Him for help?"

"God is waiting, Brett, for you to call out to Him. He cares for you the same way He did and *still* does for me, you are no different. Give it all to Him, and He will take care of it. This is too serious to handle on your own. As a detective, if there's one thing I've learned is that we can only do so much and the rest is up to God. He's the one I truly rely on."

Brett listened to Pete's words but wasn't yet completely convinced. However, he was one step closer. He began to think that for the first time in his life he may need someone *other* than himself to lean on.

"Brett, can I pray for you here right now?"

"Yes, do something," he agreed as he lowered his head. He was in a desperate state. He didn't *know* Pete's God, but his confidence in Him gave him hope that maybe, just maybe, God could save his little girl.

As Pete finished his prayer, Brett could feel himself relaxing. Suddenly experiencing a strange calmness about the situation, he felt hopeful for the first time since Adalyn went missing.

"Thank you, Pete, for everything." He smiled, shaking his hand. "I need to get back to Rachel. Call me when you find out anything."

As Brett drove home, he started to think about all Pete had said. Could it be true? He knew something different happened as Pete prayed, but he still didn't understand it all.

Pulling the key from the ignition, he sat contemplating his next move. He knew Rachel would ask him what the detective wanted as soon as he entered the bedroom. She needed to know, but how would he explain it to help keep her as calm as possible. No matter how he rehearsed it in his head, there was no way to soften it.

"Hi, honey, how are you feeling?" He smiled, standing in the bedroom doorway.

"What did the detective want?" she asked, choosing not to hear his question and perceiving from the worried look on his face that it wasn't good news.

"DNA was found at the Bennett's home. It belongs to Sophia."

"Yes," she interrupted, "it was their home. Her DNA would be all over the house."

"Her real name isn't Sophia." He sighed.

"What do you mean?"

"Her real name is Ivy Stratton, and she is a wanted criminal," he continued as he sat on the end of the bed with his head down.

"A wanted criminal?" She shrieked. "For what?"

"Rachel, please! Try to stay calm. The police are handling it."

"FOR WHAT, BRETT?" she yelled as the tone in her voice turned from alarm to anger.

She listened in horror as he explained all the details. Holding her in his arms as she cried so intently, he secretly feared for her and the baby.

After her cries quieted a little, he proceeded to tell her about Pete's prayer at the station. "I don't have all the answers, Rachel, but I'm beginning to believe that God can help us.

With her heart slowly beginning to harden, she didn't answer him.

"Do you need anything?" he asked as he slowly grazed her cheekbone with his fingers to wipe the tears from her eyes.

"I would love a glass of water," she replied, "if you don't mind."

"I'll be right back." He smiled, heading out the door.

*****

"Hello?" Rachel's mother called out as she knocked on the door.

"Hi, Daisy," Brett called back. "Come on in."

"I have some macaroni and cheese here for everyone. You can warm it up for your supper if you like," she said, handing him the dish.

"Thank you," he replied, kissing her on the cheek. "Where's Caleb?"

"He's still with his grandfather. How are you doing?"

"I don't know, Daisy," he answered, shaking his head. "We just received some bad news."

As he filled in the details, tears rolled down her cheeks. "Would you mind bringing this glass of water up to Rachel?" he asked. "I need to try and figure this out."

Upon entering the bedroom, Daisy found a disheartened Rachel crying with several used tissues rolled up and thrown all over the bed. Laying the glass of water on the nightstand, she sat next to her and stroked her hair. At the sight of her mother, she began to cry harder.

"Mom, it's bad, it's really bad." She sobbed.

"I know, honey, Brett just told me," she replied with tears continually flowing down her own cheeks.

"What are they doing to my sweet little girl? She's so innocent, Mom. She will not know what is happening to her. Her tiny body will be traumatized. I can't bear to think about it."

"Shhh! Rachel! I can't bear it either." Daisy sobbed as well. "Your dad and I have been praying continuously. God will bring her home again!"

"This feels like a hopeless situation. I can't help but think the worst," she stated as she lowered her head in misery.

"You once believed that God could help you, Rachel. Does your dog, Buster, ring a bell?"

"Yes, I was Adalyn's age, and I loved that dog so much."

"He was missing for three days," Daisy recalled. "You were sick with worry."

"Yes, I remember. I asked God to find him and bring him back home."

"You made your father and I pray too." Daisy laughed as she took a handful of Rachel's hair and moved it past her face.

"Two hours later, Buster came running up the stairs to the house. I thanked God for three weeks straight for answering our prayer."

"Rachel, He is the same God now as He was back then. I know He's not involved in your life right now, but He's waiting for you and He would love to help."

"Mom, I go to church every Sunday."

"Yes, but *why* do you go? If it's from *obligation,* you are missing the point."

"I don't know, Mom, life is so busy with my family."

"He loves you, Rachel, and He wants to be *part* of your busy life. It's something for you to think about. Try and get some rest. Caleb is with your father, and I'll help Brett with everything else."

As she drifted off to sleep, Daisy closed the bedroom door behind her and prayed silently that *her* little girl would find *her* little girl.

Chapter 17

————— ⌁ —————

Sitting on the closet floor with her back against the wall, Adalyn raised her knees to give support for her head and arms. A month had passed since last seeing her family but rarely experiencing daylight, it was impossible to differentiate between morning and evening. With daily beatings and doses of *substances* to force compliance from her, she became "conditioned" to Eric's will and only existed to please *him*.

Hearing the familiar footsteps approaching the door, she prepared herself for what came next. Once terrified of the darkness, she now embraced it to the alternative of seeing *him*.

Staying longer than any other girl, Eric had grown tired of her. Arrangements to sell her were made at a brothel where he had conducted previous business. It was time for her to go, and that time was *today*.

"Get out here," he ordered as her eyes adapted to the light. "We are leaving, and you will no longer be my problem."

What is he talking about? she wondered, not daring to utter a word. Asking questions resulted in trouble, which she had learned in the most difficult way.

Leading her to the kitchen, she found a sandwich waiting for her, and as she picked it up, he placed a glass of water on the counter next to her and instructed to eat quickly. Guzzling down the meal, she was feeling grateful due to the fact that food came but once a day.

"Go take a shower," he growled. "Dress in the clothes laid out on the bed and meet me here within fifteen minutes."

Swiftly obeying, she returned to the kitchen to find Eric standing by the door wearing a dark suit. Tapping his foot while looking at his watch, she sensed a "more than usual" impatience from him.

Where is he taking me? she asked herself, avoiding eye contact with him. She had never encountered a man so malicious as he was, and it frightened her to even look at him.

With a blindfold covering her eyes, he pushed her into his SUV and drove away from the *first* of two prisons that she would endure.

Sitting quietly in the back seat, she was aware something different was happening. This man appeared to be an upstanding citizen with his lavish suits and posh colognes. It was difficult for others to discern what a *monster* he really was. With the back side and rear windows tinted, it prohibited a person to see a blindfolded Adalyn tied to the door handles. They were unable to see a twelve-year-old girl struggling to survive an inhumane torture.

Driving for twenty minutes, she finally felt the vehicle come to a stop and wondered what was coming next as she stepped out. A warm breeze brushed over her face as she had forgotten how pleasant it was to feel fresh air. The smell of recently mowed grass reminded her of *their* neat and tidy lawn as her dad would never permit it to grow above four inches high.

With the blindfold now removed, her eyes focused on the pretty yellow and pink flowers in their window boxes and then to the dark navy door. It contained a distinctive feature that seemed to *jump* at her. Studying every detail, she memorized the red rose design etched into the frosted glass. This door was different than the others as it stood prominent to the entire house.

Eric walked carefully toward the door as to not attract attention to them, and before entering she noticed a *business* sign located on the front of the house but was unable to read it as he hurried her along.

"Hello, Eric, come in." A woman in her late forties appeared and quickly closed the door behind them. "You have brought another pretty little thing," she sneered, holding Adalyn's chin in her hand, examining her every feature.

"What is her name?"

"Adelaide, Alice, or something with an *A*. I don't know *or* care," he snarled.

"Okay, here's the payment we discussed," she said, handing him an envelope as Adalyn watched them conduct a business transaction for a human life. Her life! Just as though she was nothing more than a piece of property programmed to be a "money maker" for her owner.

"What is your name, child?" she asked, glaring at Adalyn.

"Ada . . . Adalyn," she shyly replied.

"Come with me," she ordered as she unlocked the door to a dull and uninviting room. Empty of any pictures, the dark gray walls fashioned a "cold" atmosphere, with a small lamp resting on a singular nightstand dimly lighting the space. In the closet next to her hung four pairs of pajamas in which she supposed would be used by her and her roommate. Occupying one of two "cot" beds, slept a petite blond teenage girl. Suspecting it was the result of little or no food intake, Adalyn realized that although four or five years older, this girl appeared to be the same size as her.

"This is your area," the woman snapped as she pointed to the left side of the room. "Here you will stay until told otherwise. A small meal will be provided for you once a day, and bathroom breaks come every three hours. You will service a high volume of clients and will obey my every command. I am not a patient woman, and your family will suffer if you disobey me in any way. Do you understand?"

"Yes, ma'am," Adalyn replied with her head bowed low. Thinking she was finally free from Eric's nightmare, she was now thrust deeper into a world of darkness and evil.

"Ma'am?" she spoke as her face turned a much lighter shade of grey than it already was. "I feel sick," she continued as her stomach churned from all the information given her.

"That isn't my problem," the woman yelled. "Get over on your cot."

"Ma'am?" she cried out again just as her stomach emptied its contents all over the woman's floor.

"You, stupid girl!" she shouted as Adalyn screamed from the hard slap across her face.

"Get over in your cot right now!" she demanded as she left the room.

Barely catching her breath from crying so intently, Adalyn laid curled up on the cot wishing for her mother.

"Stop that blubbering," the woman yelled as she returned with a needle. Sticking it in her arm, Adalyn soon felt the room spin as she became disoriented. Her cries quieted, and she faintly heard the dreaded words, "Your first client will be here in five minutes."

She was a prisoner! Forced to live life the way they told her to live it.

*****

Long into the early morning hours of the next day, Adalyn finally received a break. Exhausted, she had lost count of the number of men that had visited her room. Sleeping for only three hours, she awoke to the woman calling her name offering food.

Slowly sitting up, she devoured the meat and water made available to her.

"This is also a bathroom break," she snarled. "Go immediately because your work day is starting again soon."

Turning on the tap for a shower, Adalyn stood underneath the hot water in desperation for it to wash away the *scum* from her body. As her skin reddened from her persistent scrubbing, she found it impossible to become clean. Thinking of escape plans, she knew it would take a miracle for *that* to happen. "Please, Daddy, don't give up! I'm still alive, I'm not dead! Please don't stop looking for me!" She cried, but her hopes would not be dashed because she had the greatest dad and he would never give up looking for her.

"Get out here!" came a shout from the woman. "You have taken too much time."

Adalyn returned to her cot and waited for the next client to arrive.

Chapter 18

———◦C◦◦D◦———

The town of Battleford was in a state of shock over the disappearance of one of their own. Although a month had passed and still no Adalyn, everyone continued their concern by placing flyers and pictures of her all over town to help find the sweet innocent girl.

Detective Smith sat at his desk rummaging through the papers trying to decipher some *sense* of their gathered facts. He had been certain that someone, somewhere, would have called with concrete information regarding Adalyn. Many calls were made from the Amber Alert, but none led him to finding her. With that inability came his frustration, so much so that he almost tuned out the ringing of a telephone call coming through to his desk.

"Detective Smith speaking," he snapped accidently as he grabbed the receiver.

"Hello, Detective. My name is David Sharpe, and I am the owner of a gas station in the town of Maymont."

"Yes, David, go ahead," Owen replied, softening his tone a little.

"I'm calling in regards to the missing girl on the Amber Alert. I think I may have just served the woman who you are looking for."

"Can you describe her?" Owen asked, inspired by a possible lead.

"Yes, she was about 5'7" or 5'8" and appeared to be in her early fifties with shoulder-length brown hair."

"Was anyone else with her?"

"Yes, a man remained in the car. They had purchased gas and three bottles of water, but the woman paid for it all. I couldn't see if anyone else was in the vehicle."

"What was the make and model of it?" Owen asked as he wrote down the information.

"A red Ford Crown Victoria."

"My partner and I will be there within thirty minutes," Owen stated as he hung up the phone.

"Pete, let's go, we have a lead on Adalyn's case," he shouted, grabbing his keys.

*****

"Good morning, sir." Owen smiled as they entered the gas station, flashing his badge. "I'm Detective Smith and this is Detective Lambert from the Battleford Police Department. You and I spoke on the phone."

"Yes, Detective."

"How did the woman pay for everything, cash or credit card?"

"Umm, she used a credit card. Hold on for a minute, I can get you the name and number on it."

As Pete recorded the information, Owen continued asking questions.

"If you saw this woman again, could you identify her as the woman that you served?"

"Maybe," Mr. Sharpe replied as Owen produced a picture of Ivy Stratton a.k.a. Sophia Bennett.

"Ahh, I'm not sure, it looks like her, but the eyes are a little different. I couldn't say for sure."

"Okay, thanks for your time," Owen said as he motioned for Pete to leave. "We'll check out that credit card information."

*****

Upon investigating the credit card details, Owen learned the identity of a woman living in Hafford, and it wasn't Ivy Stratton.

"Another dead lead! We are no closer to finding her." Owen frowned as he rubbed the back of his head in despair.

"Let's not give up," Pete encouraged. "I have no doubt that we will find her."

"No, I am definitely not giving up," he replied. "She remains alive *in my books* as long as a dead body isn't found. She's out there *somewhere,* Pete, waiting for us to find her."

Leaving Owen's office, Pete ran to his storage locker to obtain some alone time to pray once again for Adalyn. "Please, God, keep her alive until we can find her. Point us in the right direction."

Walking back to his desk, he could hear the constant ringing of his telephone as he hurried to answer it.

"Hello, Battleford Police Department, Detective Lambert speaking, how can I help you?"

"Hello, Detective, my name is Connor Walsh, and I think I may have some information regarding the girl that went missing."

"Yes, could you hold the line for a minute? I'll let you speak to my boss," Pete replied as he transferred the call to Owen's office.

"Hello, Detective Smith, my name is Connor Walsh. My wife and I were hiking along the Wascana Valley Trail and noticed a dark blue Chrysler Sebring abandoned there. It's the same type of car registered on the Amber Alert for the little girl."

"I'm not familiar with that hiking trail," Owen responded. "Where is that located?"

"It's close to Regina, Saskatchewan. It's about a three-hour drive from Battleford.

"Did you get the license plate number?" Owen asked.

"Yes, I did, sir."

Listening to the plate number, Owen felt optimistic as he recalled Haley's information about the same two letters she had noticed on John's car that day at the park.

"This is very helpful information, Mr. Walsh. Thank you for calling it in," Owen stated, hanging up the phone.

Entering the number into the database, Owen shook his head at the findings. Eighty-year-old Stanley Powell of Lethbridge, Alberta, reported the car in question, stolen on May 30 of that year.

Picking up his phone, he dialed the number to the elderly man.

"Hello, this is Detective Smith from the Battleford Police Department. May I speak to Stanley Powell?"

"Yes, this is Stanley."

"Sir, according to our records, you reported a car stolen back in the month of May, is that correct?"

"Yes, it is Detective, did you find it?"

"Yes, a car was found at Wascana Valley Trail, near Regina, Saskatchewan, with the license plate number registered in your name. Can you describe to me what happened?"

"My wife and I went grocery shopping here in Lethbridge, and it was 7:00 in the evening, so it was dark outside. Our car was stolen within the forty-five minutes we were in the store."

"Did you talk to anyone that may have witnessed the crime, Mr. Powell?"

"No, sir, my wife and I were too upset to think about that. We were stranded in that parking lot. I'm eighty years old, sir, and my wife is seventy-nine. Who would do that to an elderly couple?"

"I'm sorry you had to go through that, Mr. Powell. We are doing our best to find the people responsible. We have to keep the car for evidence, but we will return it to you as soon as we can."

"Thank you, Detective."

"Let's go, Pete. The car was reported stolen, and I have an instinct that John Bennett is the culprit. Arrange for two officers to meet us at the scene. I'll call forensics, and I'll also get a search warrant."

*****

"Do you have any kids, Pete?" Owen asked, twenty minutes into the three-hour drive to Wascana Valley Trail.

"No, sir, not yet."

"Not yet?" Owen questioned

"Yeah, Mya and I would love to have kids," he stated, looking out the window.

"How many years have you been married?"

"Twelve, but it has only been the last two years since we've started trying."

"What happened to change your minds?" Owen asked, glancing briefly at him.

"Mya was diagnosed with breast cancer when she was twenty-five years old. She was very sick between the surgery and chemotherapy treatments that it took a full year from beginning to end. We decided to postpone having children for a few years to give Mya a chance to completely recover. Then on her thirtieth birthday, we decided it was time to try."

"That was a hard time for you and your wife," Owen stated.

"Yes, it was, and Mya lost all her pretty russet-colored hair, but we put our trust in God to bring us through it and He did." Pete smiled. "And her hair even grew back."

"You believe in God?"

"Yes, sir, I do. But it wasn't until Mya was diagnosed. A lady from a church in North Battleford reached out to Mya a few months *before* her diagnosis. They became good friends, and she invited us out to church. After we received the devastating news, we made it a point to attend every Sunday."

"Then what?" Owen asked, becoming interested in Pete's story

"We learned about God's unconditional love toward us and how He desires to be part of our everyday life. We began to believe what the preacher was saying and agreed to let God take over."

"It was the right decision?"

"Yes, Mya and I would have never made it through without Him."

"Is that what you and Brett Saunders were talking about that day in my office?" he inquired, not to be nosy but out of concern.

"Yes, I told him God can bring Adalyn back home if only he would rely on Him."

"He doesn't believe the same way you do?"

"No, he doesn`t, but I'm hoping he will very soon." He turned to Owen and smiled.

"Well, Pete, I hope God answers your prayer and brings Adalyn home."

"He will, sir, I'm believing for it."

"Do you have any children?"

"Yes, two boys and a girl." Owen smiled. "They are all married with children of their own. I'm a proud grandpa."

"Sounds like you have a big family"

"Yes, I do, and I'm soon up for retirement so I will be able to spend more time with them."

"Sounds good." Pete grinned.

"We are getting close," Owen stated as he pointed to the road sign. "Ten kilometers away."

Driving down the unpaved gravel road to the entrance of the hiking trail, they looked around the parking lot to find the car fifty feet from the entrance.

"Paul, seal off the perimeter of the car," Owen told one of the officers, "this is a crime scene."

As they sealed it off, the forensics team combed every inch of the car, inside and out, but was unsuccessful in finding anything.

"Pete, we need to initiate arrangements to impound the car. With an intense search back at the crime lab, forensics will have a better chance to find DNA."

With all necessary preparations in place, Owen and Pete left the scene and made the three-hour drive back to Battleford.

Chapter 19

———⊷∘⟨⟩∘⊶———

L ying on her cot, staring up at the ceiling, Adalyn thought about all the events that had transpired over the last couple of days. Due to the tremendous amount of stress and anxiety she had been subjected to, her legs exhibited a "jelly-like" feeling and she feared they would crumble beneath her during her walk to the bathroom.

Attempting to roll over onto her side, dark bruising evident on her upper arms caught her attention as she closed her eyes in anguish at the sight of it. Still mending from the injury of Eric's beating, her ribs felt completely crushed (although not the case) with every breath she took.

Looking over at her roommate, Adalyn heard her moans and knew exactly how she felt.

"Are you okay?" she asked as the girl opened her pretty hazel eyes.

"No, it hurts everywhere!" she answered, holding her stomach.

"My name is Adalyn, what's yours?"

"Gemma," she managed to utter.

"Hi, Gemma. How long have you been here?" Adalyn kept pumping her with questions as she needed to know this girl's story.

"I really don't know, I was fifteen when I arrived, and I think that was a year ago. When did you get here?"

"A few days ago," Adalyn replied sadly, with heavy rheumy eyes.

"How old are you?"

"Twelve."

"Twelve?" Gemma gasped. "You are only a little girl. These people are savages!"

Interrupting their conversation, an older teenager opened the door and offered food. "Please hurry and eat," she pleaded. "They will punish me if you take too long."

Gulping down the food, Adalyn took notice of the girl standing before them. With sad brown eyes staring back at her, she knew *the girl* was forced into this lifestyle as well. Standing taller than Adalyn, she appeared in her late teens with short dark brown hair.

"Hi, what's your name?" Adalyn asked, peering up at the girl as she continued to retain her friendly disposition despite her anguish.

"I'm not allowed to talk to you," she replied, feeling uneasy as she looked behind her.

"Okay." Adalyn nodded, giving back the plate.

*****

"Who's that?" she asked as the girl left the room.

"Leah," Gemma answered. "She's the 'housemaid' around here, cleaning and delivering our food. She was *promoted* when she turned eighteen."

"Promoted?" Adalyn asked.

"Yeah, she was living the same way we are now, but as she became older, they needed someone for the house chores so they kept her."

"Why don't she try to escape?" a naïve Adalyn asked.

"She's on strict supervision. They beat and locked her up for two weeks when they caught her telling me her story."

"Shhh!" Gemma whispered, putting her finger up to her lip. "Someone's coming."

As the woman opened the door, they both closed their eyes. "Break time is over." She smirked. "Time to make me some money."

Cringing at the sight and sound of her, Adalyn remained silent to avoid punishment. As men entered their room, she tried to distant herself from reality by remembering her happy life before all this took over.

A vicious cycle of clients and more clients occurred over the next two days. Men with seemingly flawless reputations and upscale careers had taken advantage of the two girls. Rich, married, and single men abused them over and over.

"Are you awake, Adalyn?"

"Yes," she groaned.

"What's your story? How did they get you?" Gemma asked as she was growing fond of Adalyn rather quickly.

Gemma listened with shock and sympathy as Adalyn recapped her entire story.

"You and your family seem close, you must miss them?"

"Yes, I do." Adalyn cried. "I miss them so much. I miss Momma combing my hair and tucking me in at night. I miss Daddy's jokes and how much he made me feel special."

"Do you have any brothers or sisters?"

"Yes, Caleb, my brother. He's eight years old and follows Daddy around everywhere. He loves badminton, and they play out in our backyard a lot."

"How did you get here, Gemma?"

"My story is different from yours, Adalyn," she began. "I was fourteen and a half and a nineteen-year-old boy wanted to date me, but of course Mom and Dad would not allow it and stopped me from seeing him. I liked Derek a lot, so I began dating him in secret. My friend lied for me and told my parents I was with *her* when actually I was with him. I fell completely in love with him and thought he felt the same way. He owned a car and wanted to take me to a fancy restaurant for my birthday. I said no at first, fearing my parents would find out, but he convinced me by promising to take me far enough away to stop them from seeing us and that he would have me back home in time for my curfew.

"What happened next?" Adalyn questioned, forgetting about her pain as she engaged in the conversation.

"Instead of taking me to a restaurant, he drove us to a house thirty minutes away from where I lived. Forcing me inside, he then sold me to a sex trafficker who beat and sexually abused me before selling me again to the woman who owns this house. I've been here ever since."

"Gemma, I'm so sorry," Adalyn stated as her tears scalded her eyes.

"I wish I had obeyed my parents," Gemma cried. "I would not be here right now."

"It's not your fault, you thought he was a nice guy and you loved him."

"It's too late now." She sobbed. "I'll never see my family again."

"What is your mom and dad like?" Adalyn asked, trying to help her to stop crying.

"They had lots of rules for me, but I know the reason for it now. They took me to church every Sunday even though I hated it."

"Why did you hate it?"

"It was boring, and every Sunday morning, I wanted to sleep in, but they brought me to church where I pretended to listen to the stories. I wish I was there now, I would not be pretending," she stated while shaking her head. "Church is a good place, and believe it or not, I miss it."

Listening to Gemma speak, Adalyn remembered *her* times in church as well, where she didn't pay attention either as she and Caleb always found something to watch on her cell phone.

Now yearning for her family, she began thinking of ways they could escape.

"Gemma, we have to try and get away from here," she stated in a tremulous voice as she kneeled on her bed in excitement despite the pain.

"There's no way to leave," Gemma answered, crushing her hopes.

"How do you know? We have to think of something!"

"No, Adalyn. I've tried several times and failed. My very first attempt resulted in a beating so bad that they broke my arm and locked me in the dark basement for a week, all alone!"

"I'm sorry, Gemma, but I can't stop thinking of a way we can get out of here, and with two of us together, we can make a plan."

"It's impossible, Adalyn, for you to even try. Please, for your own safety forget about it!"

Chapter 20

Owen unlocked his office door before daylight on the morning of the first day in September. Adalyn's case was invading his mind and thoughts to the point of obsession. What those people were possibly doing to her agonized him to his core. As the sun began to rise, its rays beamed in through his window irritating his tension headache, which he had suffered from for the past three days. Taking medication once again for it, he sat at his desk questioning where the forensics report was for the abandoned car. Three days had passed, and unable to wait any longer, he made the call to the crime lab.

"Hi, Veronica, are the results in yet for the car?" he asked impatiently.

"Yes, Detective, Dex is on the way with the report."

"Thanks, Veronica, he just walked in," Owen replied as he hung up the phone, motioning Dex to enter.

As he opened the envelope and read the results, his heart sank. Biological evidence containing two hair samples were found inside the vehicle. Ivy Stratton owned one, and the other belonged to Adalyn Saunders.

With a sick feeling developing in the pit of his stomach, Owen realized the results confirmed what they all had feared. The Bennett couple had kidnapped Adalyn. Knowing their criminal history, Owen thought about sex trafficking again. With no calls for ransom, what else would they want with a twelve-year-old girl?

"Pete, get in here," Owen shouted.

"Yes, sir?"

"The results are back from the car. The Bennetts have her. Hair samples were pulled from the car belonging to Ivy and Adalyn."

"No!" Pete bellowed. "She's in so much danger, sir!"

"We have to call the Saunders right away!"

"I'll call, Brett," Pete replied.

*****

Arriving at the station within fifteen minutes, Brett was nervous from the tone of Pete's voice and feared it was bad news.

"Come in, Mr. Saunders, have a seat."

"What is it, Detective?"

"The car which the Bennetts were driving was found abandoned at Wascana Valley Trails, a hiking trail three hours from here. Two different hair samples were retrieved from the car. One belongs to Ivy Stratton and the other to your daughter."

"What are you trying to tell me, Detective? It's *certain* those criminals have my little girl, they have my Adalyn?"

"Yes, I'm sorry to say this, but that's exactly what I'm telling you."

"What are they doing with her? What do they want with her?" Brett yelled.

"We've had previous dealings with a criminal who was convicted as a sex trafficker, and with no calls for ransom and no reason to suspect foul play because we haven't found a body, it leads us to suspect the possibility of sex trafficking."

"How are we going to find her?" a frantic Brett shouted as he paced the floor with both hands on his head. "We have to look for her! What are you waiting for, Detective? Go find her," he hollered.

"Wait, Brett, it's not that easy," Owen replied. "Traffickers are very clever, and they move fast. She could have been exchanged between several hands by now. There's a possibility they could have taken her across the border."

"No! No! No! No!" Brett yelled. "This isn't happening! This is NOT happening!"

Owen glanced at Pete with concern. He knew Brett wasn't going to take the news well, but he was actually scared of what he might do.

"Brett, we are never giving up," Pete tried to reassure him.

"How are you going to find her, Pete?" He wailed. "The detective *just* said she could already be across the border."

"We will keep investigating, don't lose hope. Remember the whole church is praying for God to bring her back home."

"Don't talk to me about God, Pete! Not now!" Brett disputed. "Adalyn, my poor little Adalyn." He wept as he slumped in the chair. "What are they doing to you? My sweet little girl." The sound of his cries indicated all hope was lost and he had given up.

Not saying a word, Pete sat next to him and waited for his friend to come to terms with the news that was just handed to him.

Finally standing up, a silent Brett walked out the door.

"He is in no condition to drive, Pete. Go follow him," Owen instructed.

As he ran out the door, he caught Brett just as he was getting into his car.

"Brett, wait, you're too upset! Let me drive you home."

"Leave me alone, Pete. I'm fine. I have to get home to Rachel. Oh no, Rachel! She cannot handle any more stress, Pete. How am I going to tell her this? We will lose the baby!" He cried again as he fell against his car.

"Come on, Brett, get in my car," Pete suggested as he laid his hand on Brett's shoulder. "I'll have one of the officers drive your car home for you."

*****

Stumbling into his house, Brett slowly walked into their bedroom trying to decide how he would tell Rachel.

"What's wrong, Brett?" she asked, alarmed as Pete walked in behind him.

"They have her Rach, they have Adalyn," he cried, toppling onto the bed.

"Who has her? Brett, you're scaring me, what are you talking about?"

"Tell her, Pete," he said crying, barely getting his words out.

"Pete, what is going on?" she asked as the color faded from her face.

"It was confirmed today that the Bennetts have Adalyn."

"How?"

Rachel listened in unbelief as Pete filled her in with the details.

"I'll leave you two alone," he said as he left a distraught Brett and Rachel.

*****

Disturbed at what he had learned, Pete remained quiet for the rest of his shift and drove straight home to do the only thing he knew to do.

"Hi, honey, how was your shift?" Mya asked as her grey eyes sparkled upon seeing him.

"It was a tough day, Mya," he replied, shaking his head. "I can't tell you about it, I just need to go and pray right now."

Walking upstairs to their bedroom, Pete's thoughts were full of the Saunders and how scared Adalyn must be. Only one person could help them now, and Pete was on his way once again to ask Him.

Finishing his prayer, Pete returned downstairs for supper but was interrupted by an important phone call.

"Hi, Pete, its Brett. Did I catch you at a bad time?" he asked with a hint of desperation in his voice.

"No, you didn't. How are you doing?" Pete replied.

"I'm not good, Pete! I need to talk to you. Can you drop by my place?"

"Yes, I'll be there in ten minutes."

"Mya, I'm sorry, honey, but I have to leave. Brett isn't doing so well. He asked me to come over."

"Yes, that's okay, I'll keep it warm for you until you get home," Mya answered, placing the meal on the top grate of the oven.

"Thank you." He smiled, hugging her tall slender physique.

*****

Walking toward Brett's door, Pete noticed him through the kitchen window. In total misery, Brett sat at his table with his head bowed low, rubbing the back of his neck.

"I can't do this anymore," he cried as Pete made his appearance.

"What do you mean?"

"This! All of it! Not knowing where Adalyn is and what they're doing to her. Trying to keep Rachel calm so we don't lose the baby. I can't do it anymore, Pete," he kept his voice to a dull roar to prevent Rachel from hearing him.

"Brett, you do not have to do things all on your own. There is someone who is waiting to help you," he encouraged as he sat next to him.

"I'm the husband and father, Pete! The one they all depend on. I take good care of my family."

"Yes, Brett, but even the toughest men need help. Look at my life, I'll fully admit that I need God."

"I don't know, Pete! I don't understand it!"

"That's okay. You do not need to understand it all. We don't have all the answers, but God does, and He will help you if you'd let Him."

Struggling from within, Brett shook his head. He wanted to believe Pete's words, but he was a man of independence and reason. A man who needed no one, until now!

"Brett, you know Mya's story," he began again. "The diagnosis she received at the age of twenty-five. Do you think that was easy for me? Watching my wife suffer like that and I couldn't take her place! It was the hardest thing I had to see, but I knew that I needed God to fix *what* I couldn't."

"Yes." Brett nodded. "I remember when it happened and how different you guys were after you made the decision to accept God. Pete, I'm sorry for what I said to you earlier about not talking to me about Him. I should not have said it because I need God in my life. I want what you have, Pete."

As he helped him say a prayer, Brett felt as though a huge weight had been lifted from his shoulders.

"Thanks, Pete," he said as they shook hands and talked some more.

"I'll let myself out," Pete stated twenty minutes later as he left the kitchen. "Give Rachel my best."

Driving home, Pete couldn't wait to tell Mya the good news. He had every confidence of God's ability to help them *all* in their time of need.

Chapter 21

—◇○C⌒つ○◇—

During one afternoon, Adalyn had lost all concept of time as she laid on her cot soaking her pillow with a steady flow of tears. Men of all shapes and sizes came to her, but the one who had just left hurt her more than the others. Standing six feet tall with broad shoulders and a heavily built shape, her tiny frame barely withstood the pressure of such a burly man.

"Momma, where are you?" She cried, rolling back and forth on her cot. "I need you! They are hurting me so much!"

As the drug effects began to wear off, Gemma was able to open her eyes, and glancing over at Adalyn, she could see a damaged little girl. Knowing exactly how she felt, tears trickled down her own cheeks as she related to the many times they had battered *her*. Recalling her *own* fighting spirit upon her arrival there, she now knew *that* spirit was "broken," a term used for girls like her—unable to fight or resist anymore. With each needle and daily beatings, she succumbed to their control. Just the way they liked it!

Forcing herself out of bed, Gemma stumbled across the floor toward Adalyn and sat next to her on the cot. "Shhh! I know it hurts, Adalyn," she said as she held her hand. "I know how it feels and I want my mom too, but all we have is each other now."

"But, Gemma, these men are big and they hurt me," she answered between sobs.

"I know, they hurt me too," she agreed, reaching to give her a hug, and as they clung to one another, Adalyn once again began thinking of an escape plan.

"Gemma! We have to try! We can figure it out and get away from this awful place."

"No, it's useless," she replied, shaking her head.

"Why not? We have to at least try!" she said as colossal teardrops fell into her hands.

"Listen to me, Adalyn! It's not going to work! My very last attempt left me fighting for my life from their brutal beating."

"Gemma, please!" she pleaded again. "We *have* to try. Maybe we can ask the girl who delivers our food to help us," Adalyn replied, ignoring what Gemma had just told her.

"Are you serious, Adalyn? She's more terrified than we are. If they catch her pulling a stunt like that, she will be sold to another brothel house to live as *we* are living. Please, Adalyn, I'm begging you, forget about it, please don't ask her!"

Suddenly hearing the door knob rattle as the key entered the lock, Gemma hurried back as best she could to her own cot.

Quickly grabbing the crackers and cheese Leah supplied for them, Adalyn decided to chance it and spoke up just as Leah was leaving.

"Miss?"

"I'm not allowed to speak to you," came a sharp reply.

"Can you help us?" Adalyn continued as Gemma closed her eyes in distress at the thought of her ignoring her pleas.

"Help you, how?" Leah asked, looking out the door for fear of someone listening.

"Help us get out of here."

"No, I can't! There's no way to escape. If they catch me, they will send me away, and I am not living *that* way again."

"Please, miss, is there a way to call my dad?"

"No, there are only cell phones here, and I have no access to any of them. Leave me alone!" she barked as she shut and locked the door.

"You're right, Gemma." She cried again. "We are never getting out of here."

Making her way to Adalyn's bed once more, memories of her mother flooded Gemma's mind.

"Adalyn, I know I hated Mom and Dad's rules for me and I didn't always listen to her, but she always made sure that I heard one thing."

"What was that?"

"She told me that God sees us wherever we are. If we need Him, He will help us, if we call out to Him."

"What do you mean? We can call out to Him?"

"Yes, I think so. That's what Mom always told me."

"How do we do it?"

"I don't know," Gemma answered, shrugging her shoulders. "Just start talking, I suppose."

"God, are You there?" Adalyn began. "We are in a very bad place, and we need Your help. Please, God, help us and please help Leah find a way to call my dad.

"Is that how you do it?" Adalyn asked as she finished praying.

"It sounded good to me," Gemma nodded.

"Now what?"

"Now we wait! There's nothing else we *can* do!"

Lying on her side with her knees raised, Adalyn tried not to cry anymore for her mom. She felt hopeful that God would help them. In fact, He was their *only* hope!

Chapter 22

———————⟢∘⟨⟩∘⟢———————

Spending most of her "downtime" sleeping, Gemma could not
bear to be alone with her thoughts due to the inability to deal
mentally with the abuse she had sustained for a year and growing instantly fond of Adalyn, she now hated to see what this was
doing to an innocent twelve-year-old girl. Like her, Adalyn too was
unable to adapt to the daily abuse, and she awoke to the sounds of
Adalyn crying once again.

"Shhh! Adalyn, I'm here," she whispered. "Try not to cry, they
will hear you."

"I can't help it! It hurts, Gemma. How can people do this to
kids?"

"They do not care how young we are! They make a lot of money
from us!"

"They're cruel, Gemma, very cruel!" She cried.

"Try not to think about it. Let's talk about something else. How
about school? Do you like it?"

"Yes, I do, and English is my favorite class, but Caleb hates it.
One summer on a family camping trip, he brought along his school
papers and threw them in the fire, One! By! One!" She smiled slightly,
remembering the good times she had with them.

"You seem like a close family. What is your favorite time of
year?" she asked, trying to keep Adalyn talking.

"Summer is mine and Caleb's, but my parents love the winter.
Do you know they even go on a date once a month?" she asked excitedly as her mood began to lighten. "On cold nights, they go skating
out on Tarrin Lake and they love the fresh air.

"They sound like a lot of fun."

"Yes, they are," Adalyn replied, lowering her head again. "Momma is having another baby, and I may not see my new little brother or sister."

"Don't give up, Adalyn . . . Shhh, listen, someone's coming," Gemma whispered as they both closed their eyes.

"Hello, Leah," Adalyn tried to smile as the young girl appeared with food for both of them.

Not responding, she waited for them to eat.

"My name is Adalyn," she continued, "and I'm twelve. This is Gemma and she's sixteen."

"I've met her before, but I'm not allowed to talk to you, guys, don't you understand?"

"Yes, we know, but we need you to help us, please, Leah!"

"No! Even if I wanted to, it's impossible."

"If you find a phone, call my dad, the number is 555-0118."

"I told you already, they have only their cells. Sorry, I cannot help you. I have to go," she muttered as she locked the door behind her.

"How are we going to get out of here, Gemma?" she asked, defeated to the whole situation.

"I don't know, Adalyn, I hope God will find a way. Wait! Did you say your number is 555-0118?"

"Yeah, why?"

"She may not remember your dad's number if she does find a phone to use, but we can tell her that 01 is an easy first two numbers and then the last two numbers, 18, are her age."

"Yes, Gemma, that's a good idea!" Adalyn exclaimed excitedly.

Hearing the door rattle again, they grew quiet, knowing it was that *time* again.

Chapter 23

Sitting in her recliner, Rachel looked out of her living room window at the flurry of snow. Now late November, it had been four months since Adalyn's disappearance. The outside temperature grew colder, but it wasn't a match to Rachel's heart. Becoming more distant as each day passed without her daughter, her heart hardened. Her precious Adalyn was gone and so was her desire and purpose as a wife and mother.

"Hi, sweetheart." Brett smiled as he entered the room, coming home from working a few hours at the hardware store. An occasional part-time job would present itself, keeping the young family afloat, but they needed him to be working full-time.

Without a response from his otherwise happy and vibrant wife, he noticed how frail she appeared as dark circles developed around her eyes. Her once warm and healthy "glow-like" complexion, now portrayed a haggard sunken look as the stress of losing Adalyn took its residence upon her delicate features. Always ensuring her hair displayed stylishness, whether up in a ponytail, messy bun, or simply falling neatly around her face and shoulders, she *now* cared not about her sense of style as her hair, with its loss of "shine," fell haphazardly down her back and was obviously unkempt.

"Rachel honey, don't give up hope," he said, trying to reassure her.

"Brett, it has been a long time," she answered with a blank stare on her face. "Too long! We don't even know if she is still alive."

"Rachel, please don't say that. I believe that she is still alive and God is watching over her until we can find her."

"She's just a little girl, Brett. She needs me, and I can't go to her. She is so frightened, I know it!"

"I know she is," he replied, hugging her. "Please, God, take care of our little girl," he prayed aloud as Rachel sobbed in his arms.

"You seem different, Brett," she observed as she looked up at him. "You never prayed before, what has changed?"

"I can't do this on my own anymore, Rachel. *We* can't do it anymore. I've asked God to be a part of my life and for Him to help us."

As tears continued to flow, she once again stared out the window. Fearing that she had given up her will to fight, Brett felt helpless and agonized over his next plan of action. Their unborn baby needed her to be healthy in body, soul, and mind, and although doing her best, depression had now *prevailed* as her zest for life vanished. Darkness and gloom enveloped her as she lived each day in defeat. Nothing or no one could convince her that her little girl would be returned, not even Brett's newfound faith.

"Rachel, did you eat anything today?" he asked, noticing how thin she had become despite the pregnancy.

"Ahh . . . I don't know, I can't remember," she replied, shaking her head.

"I'll make you a sandwich," he offered, on the way to the kitchen.

"I don't care, Brett, if I eat or not. I'm very sorry that I'm not the wife you need me to be, but I can't live a normal life knowing that she is out there somewhere and those people are hurting her. I know she's calling out for me, Brett, and I can't get to her." She cried into his chest when he returned to cradle her once again.

"I can't hold her and tell her everything is going to be okay, because it's not going to be, Brett. Nothing will ever be okay again. Even if we find her, *she* will never be the same."

Listening to his wife, Brett realized she was right. It would take a *miracle* to restore Adalyn back to the happy little girl she was, but according to Pete, God was just *that* kind of miracle-working person they all needed.

*****

"Pete, get in here," Owen bellowed.

"Yes, sir, what is it?" he answered, suspecting something serious was wrong as he watched Owen slam down the phone.

"A body of a white female between the age of ten to fourteen was found down by Landley Lake, in the city of North Battleford. I hate to say this, Pete, but she fits Adalyn's description," Owen stated with a discontented look on his face as he exhaled a long, exasperated sigh.

Becoming grieved with the thought of who it could be, Pete quickly dismissed it and allowed his faith to rise above the circumstances and refused to believe it was Adalyn.

"Call the Saunders and tell them to meet us at the Saskatoon Coroner's Office as soon as possible. I hope it's not her, Pete, but the sad part is that she belongs to *someone*. This is the part of my job I hate. Telling the parents that their son or daughter has been found dead."

Swallowing back a lump that was forming, Pete called Brett's number.

"Hi, Brett," he spoke somberly. "I'm sorry to have to tell you this, but a young girl's body was found at Landley Lake in North Battleford.

"What are you saying, Pete?"

"Brett, it matches Adalyn's description. I'm sorry, but we need you to meet us at the Saskatoon Coroner's Office to identify the body."

Dropping the phone in disbelief, Brett stood horrified, hesitant to believe what he had just heard.

"Brett! Brett! Are you there? Are you okay?" Pete's shouts were heard from a distance.

Slowly retrieving the cell phone from the floor, he proceeded to ask Pete to repeat the task. "You want me to do what?"

"I realize how difficult this must be, Brett, but it's something we have to do. Detective Owen and I will be waiting for you at the coroner's office, and we will be with you every step of the way."

Ending the call, beads of sweat cascaded down Brett's face as he contemplated on whether to tell Rachel what they were about to do. He would go alone if it meant sparing her the stress, but if it *was* Adalyn, she would want to be there.

A faint-hearted Rachel quietly reached for her coat after hearing Brett's words, and after the call to his parents, asking them to watch Caleb after school, she opened the door with quivering hands and staggered to the car holding onto Brett's arm for stability.

"Rachel, what's wrong?" Brett asked, alarmed as she squirmed in her seat trying to attain a comfortable position.

"My lower back is starting to ache," she replied, letting out a sigh. "I've tried changing positions, but I can't relieve the pressure."

"It's from all this stress!" Brett declared. "I shouldn't have told you about it!"

"Yes, Brett, you *had* to tell me, but if it *is* her, I'm afraid how I will handle it. I'm terrified that we may lose two children at the same time."

Arriving at the building, they stood at the door several minutes, reluctant to go in. Finding the courage to step inside, they found Pete waiting to take them to the morgue.

Walking down what seemed to be a three-mile long corridor, they finally entered the room where a lifeless little body laid on the cold table. Rachel gasped at the sight of a possible Adalyn lying there all alone, as she felt a "twinge-like" feeling move across her stomach.

Standing over the table, they awaited Owen to remove the sheet to possibly identify their sweet Adalyn.

"Are you ready?" he asked with a heaviness in his voice.

Both inhaling a huge breath of air, they nodded in unison for Owen to continue.

With each hand, he grasped the top right and left corners of the sheet and began to pull downward.

"Stop!" Rachel screamed, losing her nerve as the hairline of the girl's head became visible. "I'm not ready! I can't bear to look at her, Brett," she yelled, holding her stomach.

"Rachel, are you having pain?" he asked as he prevented her from collapsing. "You do not have to do this. Come out into the corridor with me and sit in a chair. I can come back in and do this alone," he said as he held her trembling body.

"No, I need to be here! I need to be with *her*, if it's Adalyn. Go ahead, Detective," she nodded, "before I change my mind."

Owen's second attempt of removing the sheet revealed a young girl with long hair and beautiful features, but it wasn't Adalyn.

"No, Detective, it's not her, it's not Adalyn." Brett sighed with relief as he shook his head.

Staring at the little girl, Rachel came to the realization this *could* have been her, and with that stressful thought, she felt a hard, cramping pain in her stomach.

"Brett, something is wrong with Rachel!" Pete yelled as he witnessed her face make a painful expression.

"Rachel, what's wrong? Is it the baby?"

"I'm having a lot of pain, Brett! I think I'm in labor!"

Chapter 24

"What do you mean you're in labor?" Brett asked as his eyes widened in unbelief. "You're only seven months pregnant, you can't be in labor!"

"Ahhh!" Rachel screamed as another contraction started. "Brett, I've done this twice before. I'm telling you, I'm having contractions, and they're about five minutes apart. We have to get to the hospital."

"Are you sure it's real labor?" Brett continued asking questions. "It may be those false contractions.'

"I don't know!" she yelled. "GET ME TO THE HOSPITAL!"

"I'll take you," Pete said as he ushered them out the door and into his three-year-old Hyundai.

"Hurry, Brett," Rachel screamed again as he helped her into the back seat. "The contractions are getting stronger."

"I'll call the hospital, Pete, and let them know we are on the way," Brett stated, taking out the phone from his jacket pocket.

"Good idea, Brett, tell them we will be there within ten minutes," Pete replied as he stepped on the gas pedal.

"Hello Saskatoon Memorial Hospital, how may I direct your call?"

"Hi, my name is Brett Saunders. My wife is seven months pregnant, and we think she is in early labor. We will be there within ten minutes."

"Yes. Certainly, sir, we will be waiting for you at the emergency entrance."

"Brett, this doesn't feel right." Rachel moaned in pain. "Something is wrong!"

"Hold on, baby, we'll soon be there, just a little further. Pete, can you drive any faster?"

"Sorry, Brett, I'm going as fast as I can, just a couple more minutes."

Pulling into the emergency entrance, they found the hospital team waiting and ready to take over, and as they helped Rachel onto a stretcher, Brett recognized a familiar face among the team. It was Dr. Parsons, and *she* knew their medical history.

"Hurry, guys," she stated as she rushed the team along. "We need to get her into the exam room."

"Rachel, how many weeks are you?"

"Thirty weeks, Doctor," she replied. "Please hurry! Something doesn't feel right. You have to save our baby!" she screamed again.

"We'll do everything we can, Mrs. Saunders, don't worry," the doctor replied as they rushed her to the exam room.

"Are you having any bleeding?"

"No, I don't think so."

"Okay, Rachel, this is Emily, the nurse who will be taking care of you. She's going to insert a catheter and get a sample of your urine.'

"Ahhh! The pain is getting worse." She screeched, harboring her stomach.

"How long have you been having the pain?" Dr. Parsons asked.

"My back started to ache around 2:30 today, and the cramping began thirty minutes ago," she replied as her face clenched in pain.

"What is her blood pressure, Emily?"

"178/94, it's too high, Doctor," Emily answered as Brett noticed them exchanging looks. "Protein is also showing up in her urine sample," she added as she began to quickly gather supplies.

"Rachel, you are showing signs of preeclampsia," Dr. Parsons stated as she too began to spring into action.

"Doctor, what is that?" Brett asked as his taut voice shook with fear.

"It's a complication during pregnancy where the mother's blood pressure is too high and she has high levels of protein in her urine. It is very dangerous to the mother and baby."

"Emily, we may have to deliver the baby. Set up an IV and give the medication for the baby's lungs.'

"Doctor, what is going on?" Brett yelled in distress, watching all the menacing events happening around him.

"Ahhh! Another contraction," Rachel interrupted. "It's really painful, Doctor, I feel like something is wrong!"

"With the pain so severe, I suspect the placenta may be separating from your womb. Rachel, we have to perform an emergency C-section right now because the baby is in trouble."

"Is my baby going to be okay?" Rachel cried out.

"Let's get the baby delivered first and then we'll go from there," Dr. Parsons replied.

"Emily call the OR and tell them we're coming!"

"No! I can't have the baby now, it's too early," Rachel screamed.

"Rachel, you have to listen to me," Dr. Parsons said sternly. "You and your baby are in serious danger, we have to deliver the baby now!"

"Brett, I'm scared," she yelled, reaching out for him as her eyes spread so wide from the fear of losing the baby.

"I can give you two a minute to decide but make it fast because we are running out of time. If you decide to go through with it, you will need to sign these consent forms."

"It's okay, honey, you're in good hands, God will take care of you," Brett assured her.

"Brett, I'm not ready for all this." She sobbed, clinging to him. "I can't do it."

"Yes, you can! *You* can do anything! Please, Rachel, I cannot lose you both!"

"I'm sorry, but we have to move," Emily cut in.

"Yes, fine! Brett sign those consent papers," Rachel cried as she frantically looked around the room, "and call our parents to let them know what is happening."

Watching them wheel his wife and unborn baby up to the OR, Brett had no choice but to leave them in God's capable hands. Memories of Adalyn's and Caleb's birth came to mind as he remembered the first time he held them. Adalyn seemed to grab his finger with her tiny hand while at the same time grabbing his heart forever. He recalled the feeling of joy when the doctor first announced, "It's a boy," and Caleb would prove to be his little sidekick at the early age of two, following him around everywhere, wanting to be just like his dad. Now they would have another addition to the family, one who they could love and spoil as well. Another chance to be proud parents. He knew this time, he had to leave his worries with God.

Unknowing what the outcome would be, Rachel knew that she needed to call out to God, so with tears rolling down her cheeks and oblivious to everyone around her, she began to pray,

"Help me, God, please help me. I need You now more than ever. They tell me my baby is in trouble, and we don't know if our little one will survive. Please, Lord, save my baby! I know I haven't followed You and I've made so many mistakes, but Brett tells me You can help us. I need to make things right with You, so I'm turning my life over to You and leaving it in Your Hands," she finished just before they arrived at the doors.

Entering the operating room, Rachel could feel her heart racing as she began to perspire at becoming uneasy and intimidated by the amount of surrounding trolley's and equipment that occupied the room. Although her third section, she would never get used to it. This time however she felt a calmness sweep over her as she watched the professionalism from each team member as they prepared for the procedure. Above the stretcher to her left, she heard the anesthesiologist and his nurse discuss the steps that would be taken to begin. At the bottom right stood a registered nurse arranging the necessary tools as another registered nurse monitored her blood pressure and other vital signs. Each with different roles, but all ready to deliver her premature baby.

"Hello, Rachel, my name is Josie, and I will be the nurse assisting Dr. Parsons with the surgery," she introduced herself as she placed an oxygen mask on Rachel's face.

"We have to put you asleep because there is no time for an epidural," Josie informed her.

Watching the anesthesiologist inject the medication into the IV line, Rachel drifted off to sleep.

With the team and everything else in place, Dr. Parsons scrubbed up, and they were ready to begin.

"Scalpel, please . . ."

Chapter 25

November 26 at 5:06 p.m., Baby Girl Saunders entered the world, but she was extremely tiny and underweight. Displaying difficulty in breathing on her own, she presented with symptoms of raspy breaths. She exhibited an elevated heart rate as well as a portrayal of a jaundiced condition of her skin.

Due to her premature condition, Josie placed her into an incubator as she hooked her up to a heart monitor along with a lot of other different tubing. With the baby taken care of, it was now time to wake up the mom.

"Rachel! Rachel! It's time to wake up," Josie called, gently shaking her.

Forcing her eyes open, Rachel felt waves of nausea rush over her from the effects of the anesthetic. Finding it difficult to remain awake for only a few minutes at a time, her alertness prevailed long enough to realize her location as Josie obtained her blood pressure.

"My baby! Is my baby okay?" She cried. "Can I see my baby?"

"Yes, your baby is doing fine, Mrs. Saunders. She is in an incubator right now," Josie replied. "As soon as you are feeling better, we will get you settled in your room and then you can see her."

"Her?" Rachel questioned with a faint smile.

"Yes." Josie smiled back. "You have a beautiful baby girl! Dr. Parsons will speak to you in your room when you get situated to explain everything to you and your husband. I will go let him know."

*****

"Mr. Saunders?"

"Yes," Brett replied, looking up to see Josie waiting for him.

"Your wife is awake now and doing fine."

"And the baby?" he asked.

"You have a new baby girl, Mr. Saunders. She is premature as you know, so her body isn't fully developed. We needed to place her in an incubator where she is hooked up to a heart monitor and some tubes. She is also receiving oxygen. This is standard procedure for premature babies, so don't be scared. I assure you, she will be monitored closely. Dr. Parsons will meet with you and your wife to answer any questions you may have."

Thank You, God! Thank You so much! I have a new daughter?" he yelled excitedly. "But, nurse, she's going to be all right, isn't she?"

"We've had a lot of babies born premature and it may take some recovery time, but usually the baby is fine." She nodded.

"When can I see my wife?" he asked, ready to dash for her room.

"She's in recovery right now, but we will be transferring her to a room in a couple of hours."

"Thank you, nurse," Brett replied as he sat back in his chair thankful for God's protection over his wife and new baby girl.

Calling their parents to reveal the outcome and to check on Caleb, Brett suddenly felt heartbroken that Adalyn wasn't there to meet her new baby sister. Knowing Adalyn as he did, he knew she would spend all her time with the new baby playing with her and trying to make her laugh. He wasn't giving up hope though. He believed she would return.

Sitting around the waiting area, he stared at the clock, wondering when Rachel would be transferred to her room. Two hours had passed, and he was getting anxious to see them.

"Mr. Saunders," Josie finally appeared. "Your wife is fully awake and calling for you. She is moved to room 8 on the maternity ward."

"Thank you," he replied as he headed down the corridor.

Walking into the room, he found a very excited mother with eyes ablaze and a radiant smile that warmed his heart. For a brief second, he recognized the *old* Rachel, the Rachel before Adalyn went missing.

"Brett, have you seen her?" she asked eagerly. "Have you seen our new little girl?"

"No, I waited for you so we could see her together." He smiled as he bent over to hug and kiss her.

"Let's go," she stated, attempting to remove the bed clothes from off her legs as she wrenched in pain holding her stomach.

"Slow down, honey, you just had surgery. Are you able to do this?"

"Yes, I will be all right, I need to see her," she replied as Brett helped her into a wheelchair.

Nearing the incubator, Rachel began to cry at the sight of her baby girl. Hooked up to all the tubing, she was helpless in her small compartment. They had almost lost her, and now here she was still fighting for her life.

Reaching inside, she held the baby's hands for the first time, allowing her to feel her mother's touch. As she did, she was reminded of the many times Adalyn reached up with *her* hands to receive solace from her for whatever misfortune she had found herself in.

"Brett, I know we had a few names picked out," she said, looking at him with mixed emotions, "but I've made things right with God, and I truly do believe that He has watched over our baby, so what do you think of the name *Faith*?"

"I think that is a wonderful name." He smiled as he knelt down beside her.

"Oh, Brett, I can't wait for Adalyn to see her little sister," she exclaimed just as both sets of parents and Caleb appeared ready to see Baby Faith.

*****

After almost two months in the hospital acquiring the special care she needed, Faith was finally ready to go home.

Chapter 26

On a mid-January morning, both Adalyn and Gemma laid sleeping. Christmas had come and gone, but they missed it. In fact, they didn't *know* the joyous occasion had passed them by. Adalyn was missing for five and a half months, and it seemed like a lifetime since last seeing her family. Her slender structure had become fragile and battered as black and blue bruising covered her body. Her healthy, long, fudge-colored brown hair was now straggly and dirty. Almost unrecognizable, her electric blue eyes were not as bright as they once were. With the sparkle now gone, it was replaced with sorrow and despair. Her features were changing from the cruelty she endured.

"Wake up, guys," Leah shouted as she entered the room. "There isn't much time to eat."

"Did you think about helping us?" Adalyn asked her as she ate the bread made available to her.

"No, I told you, I can't! It's impossible! Please, I'm begging you, don't ask me again!"

"Leah, if my dad finds us, *you* will be set free too. I promise I won't leave you behind. We can all stick together and escape this place."

"No, Adalyn, I'm afraid. I will be badly punished if I try and don't succeed."

"But, Leah, what if it *does* work, then you will be free! Free to see your family again. Please think about it. There must be a cell phone *somewhere* you can use," she begged feebly with all her might.

"I don't know, Adalyn! I'm too scared to try."

"Leah, just think about it, we can all be free from this place," Gemma spoke up. "Keep your eyes opened, I'm sure you'll find a chance to use a cell phone."

"I have to go! I cannot help you, I'm sorry."

"Leah!" Gemma called for her.

"Remember, the number," she stated as Leah turned around. "555-0118. The first two numbers, 01, are easy to remember and the last two are the same as *your* age."

Quickly locking the door behind her for fear of someone catching her, she began to think about what they were asking her to do. *No way! It was impossible*, she thought. A cell phone would never reach her hands. Although, what if it did? She would be free from this awful place and reunited with her family. Free to live again! Thoughts of escape that weren't there before flooded her mind, but no! It was too risky for her to even try.

Looking over at Adalyn, Gemma could see her half-opened eyes begin to fill with tears. Knowing what she was probably thinking, Gemma tried to boost her hopes.

"I think Leah is thinking about helping us," she whispered.

"How do you think that?" Adalyn snapped in a weak voice. "You heard her, she's too scared."

"Adalyn, don't get mad at me, I'm trying my best."

"I know, Gemma, I'm sorry, but it seems hopeless."

As the doorknob rattled again, Gemma's response was interrupted. It was that *time* again.

*****

As the day finally ended, Adalyn could hear Gemma crying.

"Shhh! Don't cry, Gemma," she soothed as she tiptoed over to her bed. "Try and think about other things."

"It still hurts, Adalyn," she cried. "I miss my mom and dad! I want to go home!"

"Me too." Adalyn nodded. "I miss my family, and I miss hanging out with Haley."

"Who's that?"

144

"She's my best friend. You'd love her, Gemma. She's really friendly, and she loves cooking with her mom. Whenever they cooked a fancy supper, they would invite me over to taste it." She laughed. Sometimes it was really good, but *other times*, ugh, it was awful." She screwed up her nose as they both laughed.

"What else did you guys do?"

"We loved swimming at the park and riding our bikes. Haley loves playing games on her iPad, but I would rather read."

"How about you, Gemma, what did you like doing?"

"I loved drawing houses and coloring them pretty colors, and the windows had to have curtains." She smiled. "As my friends were watching makeup videos on their iPads, I was designing houses."

"That's cool, Gemma."

"Yeah, it was, until I was forced into this place."

"We have to keep asking Leah to help us," Adalyn said as she tiptoed slowly back to her cot. Closing her eyes, she silently asked God to help Leah find a cell phone to call her dad.

Chapter 27

―――――⟨∘⟨⟩∘⟩―――――

"What's wrong with you today?" the lady of the brothel house shouted as she watched Leah preparing the lunch for Adalyn and Gemma. "You have water wasted all over the counter," she screamed. "Clean it up before you bring that food."

Leah had been thinking hard about what the girls were asking her to do. Constantly playing on her mind were thoughts of seeing her mom and dad. Could there be a way for her to be set free from this place? Could she risk it? If caught, she would be placed in the same position as the two girls were, and *that* thought outweighed the risk. Oddly though, the thoughts of escape would not leave her mind. In fact, the more she tried pushing them away, the more they were front and center in her mind. Quickly finishing the lunch, she made her way to their room.

Entering, she found Adalyn curled up on her cot sobbing as flashbacks of her *own* past experiences came racing to her mind. Glancing over at an exhausted Gemma, she also remembered how they needed sleep whenever possible. Feeling a twinge of compassion for the two girls, Leah was surprised she felt that way. She knew their names because they had made the effort to reach out to her, and she was beginning to feel like they were her friends. It was a vicious cycle that would continue, unless someone found them and stopped the horror.

I have to do something, she thought to herself, suddenly feeling an anger rise up within her. *I can't go on letting these people get away with what they're doing.*

"Adalyn, Gemma, please hurry and take your food. There isn't much time."

Looking up at her, Adalyn wiped away her tears and grabbed the sandwich and water. "Gemma, wake up," she called in a frail sluggish voice. "Leah is here."

As Adalyn ate, she realized that Leah had called them by name, something she hadn't done before. Was she softening to their idea?

"Leah, have you changed your mind about helping us?"

"I've been thinking about it, Adalyn, but I don't know where I'm going to find a phone," she whispered, looking out the door.

"Okay, remember the number, 555-0118, 01 and then your age,18. God will find a way for you."

Closing and locking the door behind her, Leah was puzzled at Adalyn's comment. God was never mentioned before, and Adalyn seemed confident! Maybe she *would* find a phone.

*****

Over the next couple of days, Leah continued with her chores as the lady of the brothel house kept a tight schedule for her. Finishing late brought punishment and certain privileges taken away.

"Leah, come here," the lady shouted.

"Yes, ma'am?"

"Show this gentleman to the upstairs bathroom. He needs to fix the faucet piping underneath the sink," she ordered with a look that told Leah to ensure all was locked away and no one made a sound while he was up there.

"Yes, ma'am. This way, sir," she answered as she led him up the stairs. She had earned the lady's trust with these types of circumstances. Too fearful to attempt any kind of disobedience, due to other's past failures, she followed every rule. These people ran a very close operation with absolutely no room for error.

Showing him where the bathroom was, she noticed he was an older man with gray hair. Wearing a plumber's suit, his name tag read 'Hank Manning,' Reid's Plumbing Service. With toolbox in hand, he started his job with the sink.

Finally calling in a professional to fix the leaking faucet, the lady first had every girl "silenced" so the plumber would not suspect anything.

"Leah, get up there and see why he's taking so long," the lady demanded after thirty minutes had passed, and she was becoming suspicious.

"Yes, ma'am," Leah replied, hurrying up the stairs.

On the floor, lying on his side with his head inside the cabinet, Hank continued fixing the faucet. Next to him, Leah noticed an older model cell phone, which had fallen out of his pocket.

It's a cell phone! she thought to herself surprised. *And it's one of those flip open kind that doesn't require a passcode.*

Remembering the girl's request, she realized this was her chance. With her heart pumping faster and her hands trembling, she wondered how to retrieve the phone. With a short window of opportunity here, she needed to act fast if this was going to work.

I can't do this, she thought, losing her nerve for a split second until the memory of Adalyn and Gemma's conditions came to her mind, reminding her of why she was doing this.

How can I get the phone? she questioned as her whole body now began to shiver. Spotting a cleaning cloth in the sink, which she had accidently left behind earlier, she decided to use that for an excuse to get the phone.

"Excuse me, sir. I need to get my cloth here in the sink, but *you* don't have to move, I can easily reach it."

"Okay," he mumbled, not looking up.

Taking the cloth from the counter, she pretended to drop it on the floor. Bending over, she grabbed the cloth and the phone, all in one sweeping motion.

"Oh, miss?" Hank called as she was exiting the bathroom.

He knows! she thought, stopping in her tracks.

"Can you pass me that wrench?" he asked, pointing to it on the floor.

"Yes, sir," she answered, letting out a huge sigh.

Walking to the end of the hall, she quickly scanned the area for anyone else in the house. It was all clear and time to make the call.

Flipping open the phone, she stopped abruptly, striving to remember the number.

What's the number? 555 . . . 555 . . . I'm so nervous, I can't remember. What did they say it was? Think Leah! The first two numbers were easy, Gemma said, 01 and the next two were my age. Got it! She proclaimed to herself, *555-0118.*

Barely able to key in the numbers from her shaking hands, she hoped with all her being that someone would pick up.

"Hello?" Brett answered, not recognizing the number but decided to answer anyway.

Upon hearing a male's voice and unsure if this was *indeed* Adalyn's dad, she stood motionless, staring fixedly at the floor, unable to speak.

"Leah, where are you?" The lady called out, startling her.

Understanding the need to act swiftly, she whispered into the phone.

"Adalyn needs your help, you have to rescue her! Look for a red rose!" she stammered nervously before ending the call. Unaware of the address, the only thing she knew was the red rose on the door. It was the clue used by the lady in which she gave to the clients to help them in locating the house.

Walking toward the bathroom to replace the phone, she was met by Hank in the doorway wiping his hands with an old rag. Already finished his job, he then began picking up his tools.

What am I going to do with his phone? she thought as she paced up and down the hall biting her fingernails.

"Miss, I'm done here," he said. "You shouldn't have any more trouble with it."

"Okay, sir, I'll walk downstairs with you."

As Hank and the lady discussed payment, Leah ran back upstairs to place the phone on the floor next to where he was working. When he realized it was gone, he would surely search that area.

Entering the kitchen to wash some dishes, Leah peeped out and watched as Hank searched his front and back pockets for the phone.

"It has to be here somewhere," he stated. "I know I had it. It must have fell out of my pocket while I was working. I'll run upstairs and check."

Pretending not to hear their conversation, Leah continued washing dishes as the lady looked at her suspiciously.

"It was on the floor next to the cabinet." He nodded as he appeared moments later with phone in hand.

"I hope you have a good day," the lady pretended to care as she shut the door behind him.

Breathing a sigh of relief, Leah relaxed and hoped the man on the other end of the call understood what she had said.

Meanwhile in the town of Battleford, a very shocked Brett with an unrelenting stare at Rachel stood with his cell phone up to his ear several minutes after Leah had ended the call.

"What? Wait!" he yelled. "Don't hang up! Who is this?"

Silence! The caller was gone!

"Brett, what's wrong?" Rachel asked as she witnessed a look of astonishment on his face. "Who was that?"

"I don't know," he replied at a loss for words.

"What do you mean?"

"It was a young girl. She told me Adalyn needs my help and to come rescue her. She also said to look for a red rose."

"What?" Rachel asked, surprised.

"Yeah, and then she hung up." Brett stood transfixed, staring at his phone.

"Brett! What on earth are you talking about? Where is Adalyn?"

"She's still alive! Our baby is still alive, Rachel!" he shouted, not hearing her questions. "I have to call Pete!"

"Pete, you're not going to believe this, but a young girl just called me and told me to come rescue Adalyn and . . ."

"Slow down, Brett! Start from the beginning."

A dumbfounded Rachel listened as Brett relayed the information to Pete.

"We can trace the number," Pete stated, "and find out where she is. What about the red rose?"

"I'm still puzzled at that one," Brett replied. "It's January month, where do we find a rose?" he yelled into the phone as if Pete couldn't hear him.

"It's a clue to help us figure out her location. Did she say anything else?"

"No, that's it, but she whispered as she spoke."

"Okay, I'll give this to Detective Smith right away and call you back as soon as we can."

"Hurry, Pete! We have to find her!"

Chapter 28

―――――◇•◦⟨∽∽⟩◦•◇―――――

"Please, God, don't let this be another false lead," Pete prayed as he made the ten-second walk to Owen's office. Convinced the phone call would lead them to Adalyn, Brett was ready to go bring her home. They couldn't bear any more false alarms or near misses; but now with God in control, Pete believed everything would work out for them.

"Detective Smith, we have a new lead on Adalyn's case," Pete shouted as he entered Owen's office without knocking.

"Please, come on in," Owen answered in an annoyed tone as he motioned Pete to enter.

"Sorry, sir, I should have knocked."

"Forget about it, what do you have?"

"I just hung up the phone with Brett Saunders. He informed me that he received a call from a young girl telling me to rescue Adalyn. She also told him to look for a red rose. I believe it's a clue, sir!"

"Did you get the phone number?"

"Yes, sir, here it is," he replied, passing the paper to Owen.

"That's the area code for the province of Ontario," Owen stated as he looked strangely at Pete.

Immediately entering the phone number into the computer, Owen discovered an older-looking man from Toronto. Pete listened as Owen read the information. "A journeyman plumber, sixty-three-year-old, Hank Manning, worked for Reid's Plumbing Service for forty years."

"Pete, call the airlines and book two tickets for the next available flights to Toronto. I'm calling the police department there and have them bring this 'Hank' guy in for questioning."

"Right away, sir."

"Toronto Police Department, Jane speaking, how may I help you?"

"Hi, Jane, this is Detective Owen Smith from the Battleford Police Department in the province of Saskatchewan. May I speak to the lieutenant, please?"

"One moment please," She answered, connecting the call to her boss.

"Lieutenant Richard Hughes speaking."

As Owen explained the situation to Richard, Pete was making arrangements with the airlines. The next two available flights were the red eye in Saskatoon Airport, leaving at three in the morning. They would arrive in Toronto approximately eight thirty with the time difference.

"Pete get in here," Owen shouted, "did you get the flights booked?"

"Yes, but it's for three in the morning!"

"Okay," Owen replied, scratching his head. "Go home and pack clothes for at least two days and meet me back at the station, twelve midnight. We can drive to the airport in my car."

"Yes, sir," Pete replied as he left Owens office.

"Call Brett Saunders and fill him in on what's going on," Owen shouted.

"I'm on it."

"Hey, Brett, we have some information on that call you received."

"What is it? Are we going to go find her?"

"We're not sure yet, but the cell number belongs to a sixty-three-year-old man from Toronto in the province of Ontario. He is a plumber who has worked for the same company for forty years."

"Ontario? That's two provinces away," Brett questioned. "An older man? But, Pete, a young girl called me!"

"Yes, we've asked the Toronto Police Department to bring the man in for questioning. Detective Smith and I are catching the red eye flight there tonight."

"Then what?" Brett asked impatiently, wanting them to move faster than that.

"We will know more when we get there, I'll call you as soon as I find out anything."

"Okay, keep me updated, Pete!"

"Yes, I'll keep in touch," Pete promised as he ended the call.

*****

Hank Manning sat in the office of Lieutenant Richard Hughes at four o'clock that afternoon being questioned for something he had no clue about. At the age of sixty-three, he was a model citizen, minding his own business, and now here he was at the Toronto Police Department wondering what was going on.

"Mr. Manning, a call was made from your cell phone earlier today to a man in Battleford Saskatchewan. Do you know anything about that?"

"No, sir, I don't. I started work today at 7:00 a.m., and I serviced a total of eight houses. My phone was with me at all times."

"So are you saying you *didn't* make the call?"

"No, sir, I didn't," he replied with assurance.

"Mr. Manning, we can check the phone records and prove the call was made from your phone."

"I'm telling you, Lieutenant, I didn't make any calls to that man," he pleaded, shaking his head. "I've been really busy with work all day. What is this about? Am I in trouble, sir?"

"No, not right now, but our records indicate that a young girl called Mr. Brett Saunders at 2:40 p.m. today from your number, telling him to rescue his daughter."

"What? I don't know anyone by that name, and I'm the only one who used my phone today."

"Someone made the call! If it wasn't you, then who was it?"

"I really don't know, sir," he replied, wiping the sweat from his forehead.

"Does anyone else have access to it? Or did you lay it down somewhere, in a coffee shop for instance?" Hughes asked as he laid both hands on his desk in frustration.

"No, I have it in my pocket at all times."

"This doesn't make sense," Lieutenant Hughes stated, scratching his head. "What house were you in when the call was made?"

"I'm sorry, but I don't know the addresses without my log book."

"Where is that?" Hughes inquired, placing his hand on the crown of his head.

"At work, in my locker," he replied, looking up at Hughes with his hands folded on the table.

"Officer Turner here will drive you to your place of work to retrieve it."

Returning an hour later, Hank passed the log book over to the lieutenant.

"According to this, you were at 18 Evergreen Drive between 2:00 and 3:00 p.m."

"Yes, that's correct, if the book says so. I never pay attention to the house or address. I go inside, fix the problem, and then I'm off to another job."

"It says here you fixed a faucet in the upstairs bathroom?" he pointed out as he read the information.

"Oh yes, I remember, it was a two-story house, and a young girl led the way upstairs. I noticed it because the woman who owned the house was nasty to the girl. I thought she was the maid."

"A young girl?" the lieutenant questioned. "How old did she look?"

"I don't know, maybe seventeen or eighteen."

"Could either the girl or the woman have used your phone to make the call?" he asked, casting a *this-could-be-it* look at Officer Turner.

"No, I don't think so, like I said, it was in my pocket at all times . . . No, wait! I remember now, before I left that house I did notice that it had fallen out of my pocket, and I had to run back upstairs to get it."

"Where was it?" Lieutenant Hughes asked.

"On the floor next to the cabinet where I was working."

"Where was the young girl when all this happened?"

"I caught a glimpse of her in the kitchen as I walked by. No, wait a minute!" he pronounced with his hand in the air, staring at the lieutenant's desk. "She came into the bathroom at the same time I was working to get a cloth or something. It dropped onto the floor, and after picking it up, she left again."

"You said the phone was on the floor when you found it?" Hughes asked.

"Yes, that's correct."

"Hmm . . . the young girl could have definitely used it and returned it to the exact spot afterward," Hughes surmised.

"Is that all you can remember, Mr. Manning?"

"Yes, I think so"

After a lengthy interrogation and discovering that Hank Manning was telling the truth, he was finally free to leave.

Chapter 29

———— ⊶◦C⌇⌇⊃◦⊷ ————

Prohibited sleep from a crying baby whose ears had been hurting the entire flight caused a small degree of irritability in Owen as he grumbled loudly to himself over the fifteen-minute wait they had to encounter for their luggage. After hailing a cab to leave Toronto airport, Pete remained quiet as he drifted in and out of sleep while Owen mulled over the circumstances, which led them to Toronto in the first place.

Stepping out of the cab with blood shot eyes and outstretched arms, they were unconcerned with the immense yawning noises escaping them both. With the time now revealing nine thirty in the morning, they walked into the Toronto Police Department eager to investigate the phone call Brett had received yesterday afternoon.

"Good morning, I'm Detective Smith and this is my partner Detective Lambert," Owen stated, flashing his badge, startling the front desk secretary as his robust voice infiltrated the air. "We need to speak to Lieutenant Hughes."

"I'm sorry, sir, I did not see you standing there," she apologized. "His office is this way," she motioned, leading them down the hall. "He's expecting you."

"Come on in, Detectives." Lieutenant Hughes smiled as he shook their hands.

After informing them of the information he had gathered thus far from Hank Manning, Lieutenant Hughes suggested they check out the house first from where Hank had been working when the call was made.

"We have to handle the situation very carefully, sir," Owen responded as his tough exterior softened and his patience returned, thinking about what Adalyn had been subjected to all these months.

"Yes, I agree!" Hughes nodded. "This is the address, and Officer Turner will supply an unmarked car for you."

Driving thirty minutes due to heavy traffic, they parked four houses away from the house in question and observed any and all activity surrounding the place.

"Pete, we need to get a closer look. Drive past the house to see if there's anything peculiar about it."

Slowly approaching the house, all *appeared* normal from what they could see, and Owen instructed him to drive on.

"Look, sir!" Pete exclaimed, pointing toward the house with one hand and hitting Owen with the other.

"At what?" Owen asked. "What are you looking at? Keep your hands on the wheel, Pete!"

"The door! Look at the door!"

"Yes, what about it? It's just an ordinary-looking door."

"A *red rose*, sir! It's etched in the window pane of the door!" Pete shouted, slamming on the brakes.

"Well, I'll be! You're right, Pete. Look at that! We found the clue!"

"It's the house, sir! We have it! We found Adalyn! Let's go!" he yelled, ready to bust down the door.

"Hold on, Pete, keep driving," Owen cautioned. "We need a warrant first to search the house. If we go in asking questions without one, they will have moved everyone by the time we return."

"Yes, sir, I'm just so anxious to find her that I wasn't thinking straight."

"If we search the wrong house," Owen continued, "we will raise suspicion with any brothels in the area and we may never find her."

"How *are* we going to do it?" Pete asked with eyebrows raised.

Sitting quietly, Owen spent the next couple of minutes thinking of the best way they could get inside the house without causing unnecessary alarm if *indeed* it was the wrong one.

"A sting operation!" he declared with shoulders back and eyes fixed on Pete. Hesitation now changed to determination as he proceeded to explain how they would conduct such a strategy.

"One of us will go undercover and pose as a client to gain access into the house," Owen resolved. "From what I've attained about this type of crime, they often use the internet as a means of 'advertising' the victims."

"Those sites are well-hidden," Pete concluded.

"You're absolutely correct," Owen answered. "Get back to the station so Lieutenant Hughes can help us out."

*****

At the Toronto Police Department, Owen informed Lieutenant Hughes of their plans and welcomed all advice and instructions that he had for them.

"A formal investigation is opened for this case," Hughes stated. "The city's prosecutor will direct you with every step you need to follow to ensure you successfully gather the criteria to make it permissible in a court of law."

"How do we find the information we are looking for?" Pete questioned, pacing the floor longing to get started.

"Billy!" Hughes answered. "He's our tech guy! He'll find anything you need."

"Billy, these are Detectives Smith and Lambert," Hughes introduced as they walked into his office. "They are searching for a twelve-year-old girl believed to be trafficked and need access inside the house at this address as an undercover client looking to buy time with her."

"This may take ten minutes or two hours," Billy replied. "But I'll let you know as soon as I find it."

"Let's get a coffee, Pete, while we wait, and you can call Brett to tell him what's going on."

"Yes, sir," he replied, rubbing his neck as the lack of sleep was now taking its toll.

A fatigued Pete walked sluggishly out of Billy's office. On the move since six thirty from the previous morning, his alertness was dwindling as he called Brett.

"Pete! Did you find her?" Brett answered as his usual strong steady voice crackled beneath the nervous pressure of awaiting Pete's response.

"No, Brett, we didn't but, we *did* find the house with the *red rose* clue."

"Where?"

"It's etched in the window pane of a door," he answered as Brett sensed the smile that beamed across Pete's face."

"What does that mean, Pete? Is she in the house?"

As Pete finished all the details and informed him to keep all information private, Brett pictured Adalyn home sitting next to Rachel helping out with Faith.

"Please, Pete, bring our daughter home to us," he pleaded as they hung up the phone.

*****

"That was quick work, Billy, you're a genius!" Lieutenant Hughes commended after receiving the needed information within thirty minutes regarding the location of the brothel house.

"Just doing my job, sir." He grinned.

After calling Owen and Pete, they all congregated into Hughes's office to devise a plan to walk into that house.

Chapter 30

It was a cold January morning of -18°C in Battleford, where Rachel stood in her bedroom/nursery, dressing Faith after her morning bath. Grateful the "new baby" smell had lingered a little longer than usual, Rachel smiled as she placed her nose next to Faith's head and took a deep breath in. Now reminiscing of the days when Adalyn and Caleb were brought home from the hospital, she knew how blessed they were to have such a happy healthy family. Faith was such a sweet miracle as were all her children.

Dropping Caleb off at school earlier that morning, Brett had not yet returned. Gone for nearly two hours, Rachel wondered where he could be. It wasn't like him not to call every thirty minutes to check on his family.

Her concerns dissipated upon hearing his car pull into the driveway.

"Rachel honey, where are you?" he shouted as his jubilant voice rang through the house.

"In the bedroom, Brett," she called back.

"Rachel!" he expressed, all out of breath as if he just ran five miles.

"Brett, what is it?" she asked somewhat alarmed, but his effervescent smile informed her she was about to hear *good* news.

"After I dropped Caleb off at school, I stopped at Abigail's Coffee Shop where she told me about the new construction company that had started up here in town."

"Did you talk to them?"

"I sure did!" He grinned, standing straight and tall as if he was just awarded with a gold medal. "They offered me a job on the spot! They have at least five years of contract work inside and outside in which they will need me. Most of the work is in North Battleford, but I will be home every night."

"Oh, Brett! That's wonderful!"

"I start next week, and I know our lives are in turmoil right now without Adalyn, but this is one less obstacle God has brought us through, and Pete has found the red rose that the young girl told us about!" he shouted, lifting her in his arms as he swung her around laughing.

*****

In the city of Toronto, Owen and Pete were about to embark on a sting operation in hope of finding Adalyn. Not quite certain if this was the house, all their energy was focused on getting inside, finding her, and maintaining the correct procedure so the police could arrest and prosecute her violators.

"Who's going undercover?" Hughes asked as he motioned for them to sit next to him by his computer. "We have to get started!"

"I am," Pete replied as he suddenly felt his hands sweating over what they were about to do. "Where do we begin?"

"I will message the owner of the brothel and set up a time for you." Hughes answered as he opened the web site. "I will request a girl that has long hair and blue eyes like Adalyn and will not settle for anything else."

Anxiously awaiting the reply, Pete stood, scratching his head, not able to sit any longer.

"Here we go!" Hughes stated as he read the answer aloud, "We have what you seek, but it will cost a lot of money."

Money is of no concern to me, he wrote back.

The next available slot is 4:00 tomorrow afternoon, came the reply.

"NO! NO!" Pete shouted as his voice boomed like a tuba instrument in an orchestra. "We have to go today!"

"Hold on, Pete!" Hughes replied with his hand up.

Tomorrow is definitely not suitable! he typed. *I am willing to pay double for today. If it is a problem, I will take my business elsewhere!*

Let me change some things around, came the response. *There is an opening at 5:00 this afternoon. Look for the red rose in the window of the door.*

Perfect! Hughes wrote.

"This has to be the house, sir," Pete roared, looking at Owen for a sign of agreement.

"It sounds like it," he replied. "What now, Lieutenant?"

"Now we wait until the time we hook Pete up with a wire and get him ready for the operation."

"Are you hungry, Pete? We have little over three hours before the appointment, we can grab a bite to eat," Owen suggested.

Although the last time they ate was just before boarding the plane last evening, food was not a priority for Pete. Three hours away seemed like three days, but he had to get out of the station to help clear his head.

"How is this going to work?" Pete asked as they sat in a nearby restaurant trying to eat a burger.

"Lieutenant Hughes will equip you with a wire under your shirt before we leave the station."

"Okay." Pete nodded as his stomach growled like a grizzly bear's snarl while eating its choice of prey.

"When they let you in, make direct eye contact and be confident. Tell them you have a 5:00 p.m. slot and you want what you came for. Remember you have a lot of money, so act the part. If you appear nervous, they will get suspicious."

Taking a deep breath in, Pete then let out a sigh with the thoughts of the plan taking the wrong turn. The Saunders were counting on him to do this right the first time. It wasn't the acting part involved that bothered him, but rather the fear of messing up resulting in losing her once again and probably never finding her.

"Are you okay to do this, Pete?" Owen asked, noticing him rubbing his forehead as beads of sweat oozed through his skin.

"No! I mean yes! I have to be! Adalyn is counting on me. What if I botch things up?"

"You'll be fine," Owen reassured, placing a hand on his shoulder. "Most of the Police Force will surround the place and wait for your signal to move."

"Another thing you need to be aware of," Owen continued, "it is very important that you remember to exchange money for her, *before* they lead you to her room. When she is identified and you have her in your custody, give us the signal and we will bust the place."

"Wait, sir, I need a minute!" Pete swallowed hard as he headed for the washroom.

"Make it quick we have to head back!" Owen warned.

Immediately grabbing a chunk of the paper hand towel available, Pete wiped his forehead and neck of the sweat that was now profusely developing. With each hand on either side of the sink, his head hung low and heavy with thoughts of the last five and a half months swirling around. "That poor little girl needs me." He sighed. "Please, God, help me not to mishandle the task set before me. Go ahead and behind me and help to find her. Please protect every step of this operation," he prayed. Splashing water on his face before leaving, his confidence returned, and joining Owen in the car, they drove back to the station.

*****

"It's time!" Hughes informed them. "Let's get you set up." He nodded at Pete while gesturing him to approach.

After equipping Pete with all the necessary wires and technology, they instructed him step by step with the plan of action he would need to follow. An expensive black suit, complete with gold cufflinks and tie clip, were supplied to help Pete fit the description of a wealthy client. A Rolex watch, matching boots, and a wallet full of money finalized the ensemble.

"Let's go!" Hughes ordered. "It's 4:15, and it will take thirty minutes to get there!"

"Arrange three ambulances to be standing by," Owen shouted to the dispatch officer as they left the station, unaware of what they were facing.

*****

"You'll do fine," Owen assured Pete upon noticing his quietness during their commute. "If Adalyn is in there, just remember today will be the day that she will be returned to her family."

First stopping ten houses away to allow Owen's transfer into Hughes vehicle, Pete pulled in front of the brothel. Scrutinizing the door, the red rose design appeared to enlarge to such a capacity that it conveyed the impression of it overpowering the house.

"What is he doing? Why is he waiting?" Hughes asked as they watched Pete's hesitancy to begin the process.

"He'll do it! Just give him a minute," Owen replied, thinking back upon their conversation they had about God on the way to Wascana Valley Trails."

"Come on, Pete, you can do this," Owen encouraged as if Pete could hear him as they watched him ring the doorbell.

"Hello, may I help you?" the lady asked, piercing his inner soul.

"Yes, I have 5:00 p.m. slot booked for services," he declared, remembering to act confident.

"Okay, sir, please come in."

"You have specific qualifications for the package you desire?" she asked, once they were inside.

"Yes, I do, and I will not settle for a substitute! Name your price," he ordered, maintaining eye contact and holding his vertical position to demonstrate his seriousness.

"Eleven hundred dollars cash before service is provided," she established as she glared back at him with the same type of seriousness.

Acknowledging her request, Pete achieved the transaction and stood waiting for directions to Adalyn's room.

"Leah, come here," the lady demanded, frowning as she stared with narrowed eyes indicating her contempt for her. "Show this gentleman to room 5."

"This way, sir," Leah signaled, avoiding eye contact.

"The girl you've paid for is on the left," the lady shouted, watching them climb the stairs.

"Adalyn is on your left," Leah pointed as she opened the door, confirming her identity to Pete.

Upon entering, Pete's head moved left to right, scanning the two girls that were before him. His eyes first inspected the blond girl asleep to his right. With short jagged hair, obvious of a poor attempt of a haircut by the owner, and older-looking features, he knew it wasn't Adalyn.

Glancing to his left, he caught sight of a tiny, long-haired girl. Somewhat unsure this was Adalyn, as he studied her face, he reflected back at her picture Rachel had given him. She was different, he thought, but his *gut instinct* told him, he had the right girl.

Deathly thin, with her collar bone protruding underneath a thin layer of skin and a sunken face revealing her prominent cheek bones, Adalyn looked up with bloodshot eyes and severely chapped lips at an unrecognized Pete and turned to her side. Thinking he was another client, she curled her legs up toward her chest and attempted to cry but was too weak from her condition.

"Please, mister, don't hurt me. Leave me alone," she whimpered into her pillow.

"Shhh!" he whispered, sitting down beside her as he closed his eyes and shook his head with despair. "I'm a cop, you can trust me!"

Burying her face deeper into the pillow, she was unconvinced at what she had just heard. Raising her hand, she slowly waved him away, hoping he would leave the room.

"What is your name?" he asked in a soft gentle tone, trying to gain her trust.

Perceiving something different about his voice, she removed her face from the pillow to take a closer look at him. Smiling down at her, he expressed tenderness toward her as he placed his hand lightly on her head. Although familiar, she was unable to remember who he was. As his eyes characterized a trustworthy guise, her guard relented as she decided to trust him.

"Ada . . . Adalyn Saunders," she answered in a weak voice resembling the onset of laryngitis.

"Who are your mom and dad?" he asked, knowing it was her but wanting to be certain.

Suspicious of his questions and fearing he would hurt her family, she became silent.

"Adalyn, you can trust me," he comforted as he realized her fear. "If my intentions were to hurt you, I would've done it already. I need to know who you are before I can help you."

"Brett and Rachel Saunders," she replied, agreeing to trust him again.

It's her! he thought. They had found her! It was time to move!

"Adalyn," he spoke lightly, "my name is Pete, I'm your dad's friend from church. I'm going to get you out of here."

Chapter 31

⟨⟩∘⟨⟩⟨⟩∘⟨⟩

"Detective Smith, are you there?" Pete asked, barely whispering into the wire in fear of someone hearing him.

Something is wrong with the wire, he thought, after receiving no response.

"Detective Smith, sir, can you hear me?" he asked louder this time.

"Yes, Pete, I'm here! What's happening?"

"I have her, sir! I have Adalyn! Make your move!" he stated as he swooped her up into his arms.

"Let's go!" Owen shouted, jumping out of the car. "Do you have the warrant?" he asked Hughes to ensure all was done according to procedure.

"Yes, I have it," he confirmed. "Go! Go! Go!"

Busting down doors to free the girls, the Toronto Police Squad raided the house within minutes and arrested those involved with the brothel.

"What's going on?" Gemma cried out, finally waking up to find her door open and a strange man carrying Adalyn away.

"Gemma! Gemma! We are getting out of here," Adalyn responded in a croaky voice that was so low and rough, Gemma barely heard what she had just said.

"Wait!" she protested to Pete. "We can't leave her, we can't leave Gemma!" she begged as he walked out of the room and into the hall.

"We're not going to leave her," he reassured as he waved for an officer to help Gemma. "She's coming with us, along with all the other girls."

Outside, Owen counted fourteen girls they had rescued and was sickened at the thought of what they had experienced. Watching officers cover each one with blankets as they exited the house, he noticed their arms contained the needle tracks used to subdue and control them. Brunettes, blondes, red- and black-haired girls with different hair lengths and various ages shuffled out onto the street where paramedics waited to assist them with medical care.

They had been exposed to a life of torture, assault, rape, beatings, drug induced stupors, degradation, and isolation, and would never be the same again. Post-Traumatic Stress Disorder would most likely be one of many doctor diagnosis for these young victims as they would attempt to live a normal life. Nightmares of every kind awaited them as well as the shame and humiliation they would feel once they faced life in the outside world.

Although free from this house, they would never be free of the inner struggle with mistrust of others, unless by some chance a *miracle* happened.

"Send as many ambulances as possible," Owen ordered the dispatch personnel as he watched the officers place the girls into the squad cars until extra medical vehicles arrived.

"How did you find us?" Adalyn muttered in a brittle voice, choking back tears as Pete jumped into the ambulance with her.

"Someone called your dad and told him to rescue you." He smiled. "We traced the number to this house."

"It must've been Leah," she whispered in a weakened voice. "She found a phone! I knew God would help her!" she replied in a *matter-of-fact* tone.

"Who's Leah?" Pete questioned, inspecting the parking lot.

"The girl who unlocked our door to let you in. She's our friend!" She beamed. "Can I talk to her?"

Beckoning Leah to come over after he found her with a paramedic receiving medical attention, Pete assisted her into the ambulance with Adalyn.

"Thank you, Leah." She cried as they hugged. "Thank you for calling my dad!"

"God found a way for us." Leah sobbed. "Just like you said He would."

"We have to go to the hospital now, girls," Pete explained after they had talked for a while, as he helped Leah out of the ambulance.

"Pete!" Owen shouted, running toward him, stopping the paramedics from closing the door. "Stay with her until the Saunders arrive."

"Yes, sir," Pete nodded as they prepared for their journey to the hospital.

En route, Pete called Brett to let him know they had found his daughter.

"Pete, where are you?" he asked with apprehension. "Have you found her yet?"

"Just a minute, Brett, I have someone here who wants to speak to you," he replied, giving the phone to Adalyn.

"Hi, Daddy!"

"Adalyn, sweetheart, is that you?" He cried with his voice breaking, realizing that after going through six months of utter anguish, he was finally talking to her.

"Yes, Daddy, it's me," she replied in a soft-spoken tone.

"I missed you so much! I'm sorry, Adalyn, I couldn't find you sooner. I tried as hard as I could! I really tried," he kept repeating over and over, trying to somehow express to her that he had never ever stopped looking for her.

"I know you did, Daddy, it's not your fault! I'm safe now, they can't hurt me anymore!"

"Rachel, it's her! It's our baby!" He wept as he handed her the phone, barely able to speak.

"Adalyn honey, it's Mommy."

"Hi, Mommy, is Daddy okay?"

"Yes, baby. He's just so happy they found you. I know you're hurting, sweetie, we will be there as soon as we can. Pete will stay with you until we get there."

"I can't wait to see you and Daddy!" she expressed. "Where's Caleb?"

"He's here too, waiting to talk to you," she answered, giving him the phone.

"Hi, sis," he uttered in a low-toned voice.

"Hi, Caleb, I missed you so much!"

"I missed you too, when are you coming home?"

"When Mom and Dad come to get me, I guess."

"See you then," he answered as he gave his mother back the phone.

"Honey, Daddy wants to talk to Pete again, we love you."

"I love you too," she whispered as she gave the phone back to Pete.

"Hey, Brett?"

"How is she, Pete? Is she okay?"

"She needs to see a doctor, so let's just get her to the hospital and take it from there. We can trust God in all this, Brett."

"Pete, I can't thank you enough for finding my baby girl!"

"Give all your thanks to God, Brett."

"I will. And, Pete, don't let her out of your sight," Brett insisted.

"I won't," he assured as he hung up the phone.

Approaching the hospital, Pete could see the emergency entrance becoming congested as it filled with ambulances. Stepping out of the vehicle, Pete stayed by her side as promised until they placed her into the exam room.

"Adalyn, the doctor is going to help you now, and I'll be just outside the door." He smiled as her eyes widened with fear and filled with water ready to overflow.

"I'll only be a few feet away," he promised as she tried to grab his arm in protest to prevent him from leaving.

Standing outside the door, he heard her scream in objection to the male doctor examining her, and a few seconds later, Dr. Henry Baker left the room.

"She is severely traumatized, I cannot go near her," he stated, shaking his head. "Excuse me, nurse, page Dr. Victoria Chapman stat to this girl's room. Maybe she can get somewhere with it."

*****

"Are you the girl's father?" Dr. Chapman asked Pete after examining Adalyn.

"No, I'm the detective who brought her in," Pete replied, showing her his badge; "I'm also a family friend."

"I'm sorry, I cannot disclose any information without the parent's consent. Are they here?"

"No, they are getting the next available flight to Toronto. I have their number if you'd like to call them. Their names are Brett and Rachel Saunders."

"Thank you," she replied as she headed for her office to make the call.

"Hello Mr. Saunders, this is Dr. Chapman of the Toronto Mercy Hospital. Your daughter was brought in on ambulance an hour ago, and I've just finished examining her."

"Yes, Doctor, she is with my friend, Detective Pete Lambert, is he there with her?"

"Yes, he is," she replied. "Mr. Saunders, your daughter has been severely beaten, drugged, and sexually abused. She is covered with bruising and is critically dehydrated. We need to start an IV to replenish her fluids and to treat an extremely harmful infection with a round of antibiotics."

Grieved at what he had just heard, he paused with his eyes closed and inhaled and exhaled three deep breaths before responding. "Do what you need to do, Doctor. My wife and I are getting the next flight out. Pete will stay with her until we get there."

"Also, sir, we need your consent to run a series of tests and x-rays."

"Yes, that's fine, we will be there as soon as we can," he replied as he hung up the phone.

*****

"I will let you know when you can go in to see her." Dr. Chapman smiled at Pete at the same time as Owen called him.

"Pete, I'm at the Police Headquarters giving my report, and you will have to do the same. Call me as soon as the Saunders show up."

"I will, sir," he replied as he sat in the waiting area.

*****

Two excited parents were making arrangements to fly to Toronto as soon as possible. Pacing the floor, Brett struggled with the operator as he scratched his head in frustration to locate a flight *somewhere* that would get them to Toronto.

Talking to her parents, Rachel told them all that had transpired a few hours ago.

"They've found her! Myles, Myles," Mrs. Anderson yelled to her husband, "they've found Adalyn! When are you and Brett flying out to see her?"

"Brett is booking the flights now, but, Mom, would you and Dad mind caring for Caleb and Faith while we are gone?"

"Yes, they can stay as long as you need. Bring Adalyn home to where she belongs," she stated.

"Thanks, Mom, I love you both."

"Rachel, our flights are booked for 7:30 p.m. from Saskatoon Airport," Brett shouted, hanging up the phone. "There's not much time, but if we hurry we can make it."

"I'll start packing," she announced, grabbing the suitcases.

"Were you talking to your parents?" he asked as he ran into the bathroom to place his toiletries into his bag.

"Yes, Caleb and Faith are staying with them until we get back. Faith is here with me, and she's all ready to go. Can you drive them over while I pack our things?" she replied, stuffing her tops in the suitcase.

"Yes, I'll help Caleb get ready and I'll call my folks on the way."

Running around the room, trying to decide what to pack, Rachel realized Adalyn would need extra clothes as well. With shaking hands, she packed the last of their items just before Brett called for her.

"Rachel honey, it's time to leave! We have to get moving if we are going to catch our flight."

"I'm coming, I'm coming," she shouted, running to the porch.

"Are you ready to bring our little girl home?" he asked with his hand on the gear shift.

As her eyes filled with tears, she nodded. "Let's bring our baby home!"

Chapter 32

Sitting in the window seat of the aircraft, Rachel peered out into the black firmament, which reminded her of the darkness Adalyn had just been released from. Turning to her left, she noticed Brett fiddling with the movie screen on the seat in front of him. Discerning his restlessness from longing to see his daughter, she placed her hand on his knee to give assurance that they would soon be landing. Recognizing her familiar touch, his hands dropped into his lap as he turned to her and smiled. Taking her hand into his, he gently kissed it to thank her for help keeping him calm. Looking out her window once again, Rachel battled with fears of her own of her daughter's mental and physical state.

Finally arriving, they walked into Toronto Mercy Hospital at two in the morning and headed straight for the nursing station.

"Excuse me, nurse," Brett stated, not waiting for her to look up. "We're looking for Adalyn Saunders."

"Are you a family member?"

"Yes, we're her parents." He nodded, tapping his fingers relentlessly on the station.

"Give me a minute, I'll check which floor she's on," the nurse replied, half-smiling as Rachel reached up to stop Brett's hand movements.

"Here it is, she's on the third floor, North B, Room 6. The nurse at the station is waiting for you.

"Thank you," Brett replied as they headed quickly toward the elevator.

Stepping out first, Rachel's hidden anxieties multiplied as her head swiftly pivoted in search of the "North B" sign.

"This way, Rach," Brett gestured as they followed the directions toward Adalyn's room.

Sitting in a chair, Pete was dozing when they walked in. Finding her asleep on the bed, Rachel covered her mouth as she cried with happiness at seeing her daughter.

"Adalyn honey, it's Mommy," she stated in a low soft voice to help prevent from startling her. "Wake up, sweetie, your dad and I are here," she continued, sitting next to her, gently shaking her foot.

"NO! Don't touch me!" she screamed as she tried batting Rachel away, believing she was still dwelling at the brothel. "Get away from me!"

As her head swiveled at Brett, Rachel sprang into *"mom"* mode and quickly consoled her frightened daughter.

"Adalyn, it's Mommy, no one is going to hurt you!" she soothed, but as Adalyn turned over and removed the bed covers to reach up to her mother, Rachel gasped as she witnessed Adalyn's concaved stomach with her ribs protruding outward. Covering her limbs were a mixture of old yellow bruising, outlined with dark gray rings from previous beatings, along with several fresh wounds consisting of deep purple and black contusions. Her normal pinkish skin was discolored and swollen from all her injuries.

"Mommy?" she questioned as her eyes adjusted to the light.

"Yes, baby, it's me, it's Mommy!"

"Mommy, I've missed you," she cried, jumping up and clinging to Rachel. "I called out for you and begged Daddy to save me, but you couldn't hear me." She sobbed.

"I know, sweetheart, we are so sorry you had to go through all that." She cried also as she rocked Adalyn in her arms. "You're safe now, and your dad is here too."

"Daddy!" she whimpered as she reached up for him. Tightly hugging her, he refused to let her go, for fear of someone robbing her again

"It's okay, Daddy." She smiled slightly as he finally released her.

"I've missed you so much, pumpkin. I'm sorry for letting you go to that bookstore."

"I called out to God, Daddy. I asked Him to help Leah find a phone, and He did, Daddy! He helped you find me!"

"I know He did, Adalyn." He hugged her again as tears trickled down his face.

Watching the reunion, Pete choked back his own tears as he heard their heartbreaking conversation. He was so grateful to God for helping him walk into that brothel to save Adalyn and those girls from a "trafficked" lifestyle. She had now become like his own daughter, and he would be a third set of eyes watching out for her safety.

"Thank you, Pete, for all you've done." Brett smiled, shaking his hand as he wiped his face of the tears.

"No thanks are required, Brett! I'm glad Adalyn is found."

"Yes." Brett nodded, looking over at her. They had a lot to be thankful for.

"You've had a long two days, Pete. Why don't you go and get some rest," Brett suggested.

"Yeah, that sounds like a good idea," he agreed, rubbing his neck. "Before I go though, I wanted to let you know that Detective Smith will be here in the morning to get a statement from her."

"Okay." he frowned as he rubbed his chin. "I understand. Rachel and I will be expecting him."

"Adalyn, since your parents are here, I'm going to leave and get some sleep." Pete softly smiled at her as he walked over to the bed.

"Thank you, Pete, for staying with me," she replied, extending her hand toward him as he gently touched it to say goodbye.

"Call my cell if you need anything," he added as he left the room.

*****

Awakened by a knock on the door early the next morning, Brett and Rachel were greeted by the doctor who examined Adalyn the previous evening.

"Good morning, Mr. and Mrs. Saunders, I'm Dr. Victoria Chapman," she stated, shaking both their hands. "How's Adalyn this morning?"

"She's sleeping still," Rachel replied. "What is your diagnosis, Doctor?"

"Could I speak to you outside please," she motioned, heading toward the door.

"Your daughter has suffered a very traumatic experience," Dr. Chapman began. "We had to run a series of tests and x-rays for this sort of crime as you know. Physically, she is starting to recover. Her electrolytes are returning to a safe level, and her blood pressure is back to normal. She will have to stay here another five days until the IV antibiotics have finished their course. Also, we need to perform the necessary drug withdrawal protocol, and she will need rehab when you return to your hometown.

"Yes." They both nodded as they listened intently.

"The bruising will heal and x-rays show no broken bones, but there is evidence that her ribs were broken and healed sometime during the ordeal."

"How could someone do this to a little girl?" Rachel cried as she placed her hand to her mouth.

"I don't know, Mrs. Saunders," Dr. Chapman replied, touching her arm in sympathy. "Adalyn is going to need a great deal of support," she continued. "The emotional scars she has right now may take a significant time to heal, but she is young, and with the right therapy, she can overcome this. She will need a lot of time to adjust to what has happened to her, so be patient and understanding. She has a long road of recovery ahead of her."

"Oh, Brett," Rachel screeched, "what has happened to our little girl?"

"Where do you live?" Dr. Chapman asked, trying to be sensitive to the situation

"Battleford, Saskatchewan," Brett replied as Rachel cried in his arms.

"I know a good therapist in North Battleford, I'll call and set up an appointment for you when you return home."

"Thank you, Doctor," Brett responded as she left them.

"Brett, is our baby going to survive this mentally?"

"Yes, Rachel, with God's help, she will! He helped us to find her, and He'll definitely restore our Adalyn back to us again."

"When should we tell her about Faith?" she asked as she began to feel hopeful.

"It looks like she's awake, we can tell her now if you want."

*****

"When can we go home?" Adalyn asked, sitting up in bed as they entered back into the room.

"As soon as the antibiotics are finished," Rachel replied.

"How much longer will that be?"

"Five days," Brett answered.

"Five more days? That's a long time," she groaned. "I want to go home soon, Daddy."

"I know you do, but you need the medicine to help you get better. Your mom and I will be with you the entire time."

"Okay, Daddy," she agreed, "as long as you and Momma stay with me."

"Adalyn, your dad and I have some good news to tell you."

"What is it?" she asked as her tone perked up.

"You have a new baby sister. Her name is Faith."

"A baby sister?" She lowered her head as her eyes welled with tears.

"What's wrong, honey?"

"I wanted to help you before she was born. I wasn't even there when you brought her home from the hospital." She cried, flopping back down on her pillow as she turned away from them. "I've missed out on so much."

"It's all right, Adalyn. Everything has worked out, and you can see her when we get back home."

Refusing to answer, she buried her head into the pillow as Brett and Rachel looked at each other. Knowing she needed time to adjust

just as Dr. Chapman had said, they let her cry without questioning her behavior.

*****

Arriving an hour later, Detective Smith visited the Saunders to obtain Adalyn's statement. Although extremely difficult for her to rehash the whole event, she remembered each and every detail without fail. It was a lengthy statement, but she didn't care. Those people needed to be stopped for the horrible things they were doing. Brett paced the floor as he rubbed his head, ready to make a run for it, due to the inability to listen to what they had done to his princess, while Rachel sat in the chair fidgeting, crying as quietly as she could as they heard the horrific elements coming from their daughter.

"I'm sorry, Detective," Brett interrupted as he observed Adalyn's face lose the little bit of color she was regaining, and her eyes glaze over with the memories fresh in her mind. "She's had enough, I need you to stop," he stated as she turned away from them and laid back down.

"Yes, that's fine, I think I have all that I need," Owen stated as he put his notebook away. "You're a brave girl, Adalyn," he continued. "I'm sorry I had to do this, but with the information you have given me, it will bring us closer to catching the people who did this to you. I'll see myself out," he stated as he left the room.

*****

Over the next few days, Brett and Rachel spent the time talking to Adalyn reminding her of the good times they had as a family. Listening to how God had saved Faith's life, Adalyn was thankful once again for all His help. They laughed as Rachel recalled the time when Adalyn and Caleb had prepared breakfast in bed for her on Mother's Day. Burning the bread, they set off the fire alarm, awakening a frightened Brett as he jumped up to shut it off. "Even though the bread was black"—she laughed—"I ate it anyway thanking you with every bite."

*****

Finally, ready to go home after six days in the hospital, Dr. Chapman signed the release papers as Brett made the necessary arrangements with the airlines.

Awaiting her homecoming, two sets of grandparents, Caleb, and Faith were present to welcome them home.

Overwhelmed by all the attention, Adalyn burst into tears and buried her face into her mother's stomach.

"It's okay, Adalyn, I'm here," Rachel soothed. "You don't have to be afraid."

"Sis, I'm so glad you're home! I missed you a lot!"

Upon hearing his voice, she slowly turned and faced Caleb. Running toward her as she smiled at him, he wrapped his arms around her waist. "I love you!" He squeezed.

"I love you too," she whispered as she hugged him back.

Too difficult to face everyone, she barely kept her head up as she slowly walked toward her grandparents. Unable to make eye contact, she managed to hug each person individually. Understanding the circumstances, they allowed her to have some time to adapt.

Sitting on the living room couch, she stared out the window for the longest time incapable to talk or do anything except sit.

How long was it going to take for her to be back to normal? A very long time, they feared.

Chapter 33

U nable to sleep, Rachel glanced at the clock as it read 2:20 a.m. Returning to her wide-eyed gaze up at the ceiling, she listened to Brett's loud snoring that had kept her awake up until now. "Ugh!" She moaned as she turned her face into her pillow to help drown out his snoring.

Adalyn had been home for two days, but she wasn't the same Adalyn. Disappeared was her interest in reading as daily she laid quiet and distant on her bed.

"Stop! Don't touch me! Leave me alone!" Adalyn's deafening cries rang through the house into the early morning hours. Upon hearing her daughter, Rachel sprang to her feet and ran to her room. Quickly switching on the light, she discovered Adalyn thrashing about her bed and yelling out to the person present in her nightmare.

Sitting beside her, Rachel found her in a pool of sweat as she gently awakened her. "Adalyn, honey, wake up! You're having a bad dream!"

Scanning the room as she opened her eyes, Adalyn fell into her mother's arms weeping.

"I was dreaming, Mommy! I was in that awful house, and they were hurting me!"

"Shhh! I'm here," Rachel whispered, rubbing her back. "There's no one here to hurt you."

"I'm afraid to go back to sleep," she cried, clinging to her mother. "Will you stay with me?"

"Yes, sweetheart, I'll stay by your side for the rest of the night," she promised as she stroked her hair, and by the sound of her mom's gentle voice, Adalyn realized that for the first time in six months, she does not have to be afraid anymore. She is finally in the safety of her mother's arms as she drifted off to sleep.

Dear Lord, please help my baby, she silently prayed. *Please keep the nightmares away and help her to recover.*

*****

Sunshine and bitter cold temperatures greeted them early the next morning. Awakened by Faith's hunger, Rachel had been on the move for hours and was feeding her when Adalyn made an appearance into the kitchen.

"Hi, Momma," she mumbled as her eyes navigated toward the floor.

"Good morning, sweetie, do you want some breakfast?"

"I'm not very hungry," she replied quietly.

Placing Faith in her bassinette, Rachel prepared cereal at the kitchen counter for Adalyn as she sat at the table with her head down. Withdrawn, she wasn't her usual chipper self anymore, and no matter how much Caleb tried talking to her, she barely acknowledged him or Faith.

"Try to eat some cereal, honey," Rachel probed, laying the bowl in front of her.

Watching from the corner of her eye, she spotted Adalyn picking up the spoon and taking little sips. Hardly fed while away, her body became accustomed to insufficient amounts of food so much so that she found it difficult to swallow any food her mom gave her.

"Adalyn honey, please try and eat, you need some nourishment."

"I'm trying, Momma!" she screamed, slamming the spoon onto the table. "It's making me sick, you don't understand!"

Running to her side after realizing what she had just said, Rachel tried reaching out to her, but to no success.

"Leave me alone!" she cried, pushing her away as she ran for her room.

"What's going on?" Brett asked, entering the house, just in time to see Adalyn run off.

"I don't know how to help her, Brett." Rachel burst into tears as she shook her head. "Our daughter needs so much love and care, but she is *unable* to accept it. I keep saying the wrong things. I don't know what to do."

"We have to take this one step at a time," he explained, taking her into his arms. "She *will* get through this, Rachel. God has brought her back home to us, and He will help her heal."

Heartbroken, she agreed and returned to the sink to wash the breakfast dishes. Feeling helpless, she knew she had to leave the hard stuff to God. He was the only one who could completely make her whole again.

*****

Making progress after a two-week time frame, Adalyn was able to eat small portions without becoming nauseous. Now present at the dinner table for every meal, she had gained one pound and was climbing.

*****

It was one of those Saturdays when the winter air and snow were so inviting that one had to go out and enjoy. Immediately after lunch, Caleb convinced Adalyn to go outside to make a snowman, making Rachel a very happy mom. Watching from the living room window, her eyes filled with tears as she noticed the "twinkle" returning to Adalyn's eyes.

Throwing a snowball at Adalyn, Caleb turned and ran for fear of her returning *ten* snowballs to his one, as Rachel laughed, on-looking their afternoon of fun. "Thank You, God," she whispered under her breath.

Bursting through the door with mounds of snow on their winter boots, they had completed their outside fun and was now removing their outerwear. Quickly melting from the heat of the house, the snow formed puddles of water all over Rachel's clean floor. Normally, she would've scolded such behavior from them, but not today. This time she welcomed it! What a change had occurred within Rachel as well. Little things that she had taken for granted and even was annoyed with, *now* were a joy to her. Cherishing every day with her family was now a priority.

"I'm leaving for the grocery store, do anyone want to go with me?" Rachel asked.

"Where's Dad?" Caleb inquired as he came running from his room.

"He's out in the shed fixing the broken runner on your sled."

"Can I stay here with him?" Caleb answered, looking up at her with his big brown doe eyes.

"Yes, of course you can."

"I'll go," Adalyn replied hesitantly, unsure if she was making the correct decision.

"I'll grab my purse, and we can leave as soon as your dad comes in to stay with Caleb and Faith." She smiled.

*****

Pulling into the grocery store parking lot, Rachel observed the copious amount of vehicles which occupied the large area. Fearing the crowd of people would upset Adalyn, Rachel was reluctant to step out.

"Are we going in, Momma?" she asked innocently, looking at her mother with eyebrows raised, confused as to why they had remained in the car.

"Yes, let's go," she answered, suspecting Adalyn was doing fine.

Taking a shopping cart, they headed for the vegetable section and began filling it with lettuce, tomatoes, and broccoli as Adalyn turned up her nose at the thought of eating them.

Now proceeding for the meat section, a strong whiff of a male's cologne met them. Upon breathing it in, Rachel sneezed three times causing her to laugh as she looked at Adalyn for the same response.

Staring past Rachel, Adalyn stood frozen, unable to move as her formally reddened cheeks from spending the afternoon outside in the brisk winter atmosphere turned colorless. Shaking from head to toe, Adalyn had been affected severely by this.

"Adalyn, it's Mommy! Look at me, sweetie! What's wrong?" she questioned, kneeling down in front of her as to look directly into her eyes.

"Th-That smell!" she stammered. "It's the same smell as that first man. He was so mean, Momma!"

"It's okay, don't be frightened!" Rachel comforted, reaching for her and hugging her tight. "That was Tom, the Produce Manager. There's no one here to hurt you." *Oh God, You've brought her this far, please help her get through this. Don't let her have a setback!* she prayed silently.

"How about if we skip the groceries?" she suggested as Adalyn settled into her arms. "Let's go across the street and get some ice cream." She smiled cheerfully as Adalyn nodded slowly.

"Momma, do you mind if we go home instead?" she asked, turning toward Rachel as they left the store. "I'd like to see Faith."

"Sure thing, honey, I think that's a great idea." She grinned.

Returning home, they found Brett and Caleb elbow-deep in assembling a Robotics Kit, with pieces strung all over the table, while Faith in her pretty coral sleeper napped soundly beside them in her bassinette.

"Here's my two other favorite girls." Brett smiled as they walked into the house.

"Hi, Daddy." Adalyn smiled as she perked up again. "What are you guys doing?"

"We're trying our best to put this robot together." He laughed. "But I don't think we are doing very well."

Wrapping her arms around his neck, she gave him a heartfelt hug.

"What's this for?" he asked as he turned facing her to hug her back.

"I love you, Daddy," she answered in an appreciative tone.

"I love you too, sweetheart."

"Momma, can I feed Faith this time?" she asked, hearing her stir in the bassinette.

Handing her the bottle, Rachel beamed as she watched Adalyn feed Faith. Suddenly, strongly aware of the fact that Adalyn was going to be okay, she wiped her tears and whispered a prayer of thanks to God for all He had done.

*****

As the months passed and snow melted, the cold winter days were quickly disappearing as the temperatures rose. With longer April days, the sun's brilliance illuminated the evening's darkness thereby encouraging the family's temperament.

Two months of therapy proved to be effective and a positive asset for Adalyn as she adapted to her normal life again. Requesting to meet with Brett and Rachel alone one morning, her therapist waited in her office for them to arrive.

"Good morning, Mr. and Mrs. Saunders, I'm so glad you could both join me this morning." She smiled, shaking their hands.

"Good morning," they both answered simultaneously.

"I've asked to meet with you this morning to discuss Adalyn's progress," she stated, inviting them to sit.

"Yes, we feel like she is becoming more and more of our happy little Adalyn as each day passes," Brett replied. "And she doesn't have as many nightmares anymore."

"You are correct, Mr. Saunders." She nodded in agreement. "In fact, she is doing remarkably well, better than I had expected."

Cognitive of the reason why, Brett and Rachel smiled as they looked at one another.

"Well, Doctor, we have God to thank for that!" Rachel replied.

"Yes, I believe it *is* a miracle, because it's too difficult to comprehend that a young girl who has experienced such trauma in her life has bounced back so quickly. I plan to clear her for school in the fall."

"That's wonderful news, Doctor!" Rachel smiled, knowing her family was going to be back to normal.

"Thank you, Doctor," Brett stated, shaking her hand before they left her office.

*****

Sitting at the kitchen table, Mr. and Mrs. Saunders were enjoying a cup of coffee when Brett and Rachel walked in.

"Hi, Mom and Dad," Brett greeted, kissing his mother on the cheek. "Thanks for babysitting."

"Your welcome, son," Mr. Saunders replied. "Glad to do it."

"How was the meeting?" Mrs. Saunders asked as she laid her cup on the table.

"Adalyn is doing really well. The doctor is pleased with her progress," Rachel answered before reaching for Faith's rattle to try and make her laugh.

"That's great news!" She smiled.

"She also plans to clear her for school in the fall," Rachel continued as she picked up Faith into her arms." Where *is* Adalyn?"

"She's in her room now," Mrs. Saunders answered. "She's a little quieter than usual this morning."

"Is she okay?" Rachel asked, handing Faith to Brett before heading in her direction.

"Adalyn, sweetie, what's wrong?" she asked, concerned after finding her crying on her bed.

"Momma, there are other girls like me," she cried. "Trapped in those houses, like I was. There are men hurting them every day, and they have no one to help them. I know how hard it is for them, and I feel so bad. I want to help them, Momma, just like God helped us."

Unable to process what she had just heard, Rachel sat quietly thinking. How could a twelve-year-old girl, who had just been freed from that torture, even think about returning. Putting that time behind her and forgetting what had happened was what Rachel thought Adalyn was doing; but as she continued to think about it, she realized she would not have expected anything else from *her* Adalyn. With God healing her from every perspective, she was indeed an exceptional girl, whose desire now was to help other girls escape the horror she had herself endured.

"Adalyn, it was really bad what happened to you, but I understand your kindness to want to help others in the same situation." Rachel smiled as she embraced her. "God has made you a very special girl, and I believe that one day, with *His* help, you will save girls who are trapped into that same type of lifestyle."

"Momma, I forgive all those people that hurt me, and God will forgive them too if they are truly sorry for all that they did."

"Yes, Adalyn, He will. You have a good heart."

Astonished at her daughter's words, Rachel closed her eyes in thankfulness, knowing that God had taken care of *everything!*

*****

Pulled over for speeding six months later, in Hamilton, Ontario, Lawrence Moore and Ivy Straton, a.k.a. John and Sophia Bennett, were taken into police custody after the officers performed a license plate check on the stolen vehicle they were driving. Discovered as wanted criminals, they were arrested and sentenced to serve many years in federal prison. Their cooperation with the police led to the arrest and conviction of all who were involved in Adalyn's case.

Sleeping much better with the knowledge that her abductors were put away for a long time, Adalyn knew she could move past it.

Now, however, she wanted to help others escape from what *she* had escaped from herself. Once dreaming of becoming an English professor, she now realized that God had other plans for her life, and she was willing to wait for His timing.

Author's Note

Writing this novel was a very difficult challenge and I struggled in doing so because of the heinous crime of sex trafficking!

Although this book is fictional and written on a smaller scale, it is an example of what these victims have to endure. The harsh reality is that people like Adalyn are exploited and traumatized in a much more violent way than I have portrayed in the book!

Even though some of the pages of this novel maybe hard to read, please remember that these young people have to live it!

If you are reading this novel and have been a victim of this type of crime, I can't even imagine or comprehend the pain that you have been through or that you are carrying, but please know that God loves you and He can heal your pain.

I hope this enlightens people to this wickedness and maybe inspire others to join in and help take action in stopping the vicious cycle of trafficking.

About the Author

———◦◦◦◦———

L isa is employed as a licensed practical nurse and was born and raised in a small town in the province of Newfoundland.

She enjoys the outdoors, spending time with family and friends, and is involved with women's ministries at her local church.

From an early age, it has been a dream of Lisa to write a book, and with God's help and inspiration, that dream was fulfilled in *Snatched from Innocence*.

CPSIA information can be obtained
at www.ICGtesting.com
Printed in the USA
LVHW110349160519
617865LV00005B/7/P

9 781643 492865